The Purpose of Erie
Banking On It

Jane Neagley

The Purpose of Erie
Banking On It

Jane Neagley

The Purpose of Erie - Banking On It

Copyright 2026 by JaneNeagWrites

www.janeneagwrites.com

ISBN: 979-8-9990352-2-6

Cover Art by RD Creative Strategy

Interior Design by Megan Wilbur

Editing by Elyssa Warkentin | www.elyssawarkentin.com

"Hey Doc! Where you goin' now?
Back to the Future?"
"Nope. Already been there."

- *Marty McFly & Doc Brown*

Chapter 1

Part 2
October 1987

Cassidy bounced her leg underneath her desk. The sounds of yelling could be heard across the entire office. Her stomach churned. She knew what was happening. Everyone in the office knew what was happening. Devon Parks was getting fired. Cassidy always imagined that this would be a joyous occasion. However, the reality was far different. Devon wasn't being let go for being an asshole, or even a bad accountant. He was annoyingly good at his job. He was being terminated because the company was failing. While Cassidy appreciated still being employed, watching her coworkers being picked off one by one was not something she relished.

Devon wasn't going down without a fight. After almost ten minutes of yelling, Mr. Jelif's door swung open and Devon stormed out. Everyone avoided his gaze and focused completely on their work. Everyone except Cassidy, who watched as Devon went to his desk, grabbed his jacket, keys, and a framed picture off his desk before turning to go. He caught Cassidy watching him and paused.

"Bet you're fucking thrilled," he said sharply.

"I'm not," Cassidy replied honestly. They stared at each other for a long moment. The air was heavy.

"I actually believe you."

"Good luck."

"Your days are numbered, Banker. Don't be an idiot," Devon said before nodding and walking out the door. Cassidy's heart gave a weird thump. Today sucked.

After work, Cassidy walked two blocks to the corner sub shop where she was meeting Jake for an early dinner. The little bell jingled as she opened the door, and she smiled as she spotted Jake sitting at the first booth.

"Hey," Cassidy greeted cheerfully, leaning down to give him a quick peck on the lips before taking a seat across from him.

"Hi! Let me put these away," Jake said, gathering up the papers sprawled out on the table in front of him.

"Grading?" Cassidy asked, snatching one of the test papers to read.

"Yes. Gave a test this morning. I like to get them back quickly so we can review and they can ask questions before we move on," Jake said.

"Wow," Cassidy said, eyeing an equation. "I actually understand some of this."

"I imagine you would." Cassidy handed the test back so he could return it to his bag with the others.

"Other than the test, how was your day?"

"Pretty uneventful. Yours?"

"Ugh," Cassidy groaned.

"Uh oh..."

"Devon got fired."

"I thought you'd be happy about that!"

"Not when it happened like this."

"Fair enough," Jake agreed.

"This whole situation just sucks."

"It does."

"Let's put our order in. Maybe food will help me think straight," Cassidy sighed.

They placed their orders, a meatball sub for Jake and a chicken caesar wrap for Cassidy, and returned to their booth with two bottles of pop.

"Do you have any plans this weekend?" Cassidy asked, taking a sip of her 7Up.

"Nothing specific. I was hoping we could get together at least once," Jake said, his smirk going right through her.

"Definitely."

"Did you have something in mind?"

"Well…" Cassidy fidgeted in her seat. "I was wondering if you would like to come for dinner at my parents' house?"

"Meet your parents?" Jake looked surprised, but not in a bad way.

"Yeah, and my brothers, at our monthly family dinner."

"Oh, wow!"

"It's really nothing fancy, we just all meet at mom and dad's and have a few hours together."

"And they want me there?"

"I'm sure they will," Cassidy smiled.

"Huh?"

"I didn't ask my mom yet, but I am ninety-nine point nine percent sure that she will be over the moon. I just wanted to see if you were interested, first. Because my mom would be very upset if I said I was bringing a boyfriend home and then he didn't show," Cassidy explained.

"Cassidy, of course I want to meet your parents! I'm a little nervous about meeting your brothers, especially since Alex wasn't super thrilled with me, but really, yes, I want to be there."

"Great!" Cassidy leaned over the table to kiss him. "I'll call mom tonight and tell her."

"I can't wait."

Chapter 2

"Hello?"

"Hi, mom."

"Hi Cassidy, darling," Lynne hummed.

"How are you?"

"Good. I just finished baking all the cookies and now I'm just wiping down the kitchen."

"Why are you baking cookies?" Cassidy asked.

"Because tomorrow evening is Back to School night and the principal makes me give an address to all the parents about the nurse's office and what the process is when the kids need to be sent home, and all that jazz."

"Yeah?"

"And well, I find that parents are far less whiny and angry at me if I have cookies to offer them," Lynne explained.

"Smart."

"I thought so."

"But wouldn't it be smarter to just have a plate of carrots and dip to show the parents you're promoting health food?" Cassidy suggested.

"Dammit," Lynne sighed, making Cassidy laugh.

"Sorry, mom."

"Well, maybe next year. I'm not leaving your father with six dozen cookies!"

"Poor dad," Cassidy said, smiling into the receiver.

"Not 'poor dad!'"

"You can freeze the cookies," Cassidy pointed out.

"Your father knows how to open the freezer. That's a no-go."

"Fair enough."

"How are you, sweetie?" Lynne asked, changing the subject.

"I'm alright."

"Alright?"

"Yes, yes."

"Cassidy, you don't usually call in the middle of the week just to say you're alright," Lynne noted. Cassidy swallowed. Her mom knew her too well.

"Well, um… okay… so, I just thought I should tell you… that, um… I have a new boyfriend."

"Oh, really?"

"Yes. And, well, it's going well, and I was thinking… that, well, maybe I could bring him to our dinner this Friday," Cassidy said haltingly. There was a bit of a pause, and Cassidy bit her bottom lip.

"Seriously?" Lynne asked excitedly.

"Yes?"

"Well, yes, we would love to have him here!"

"Great! Thanks, mom!"

"So…"

"So…" Cassidy mimicked.

"Are you going to tell me anything about this boyfriend, or will I just be surprised like everyone else at the end of the week?" Lynne asked.

"Oh, um, yeah… his name is Jake. He works at Mercyhurst," Cassidy said.

"What does he do there?"

"He's a professor."

"Seriously?" Lynne sounded shocked.

"Why are you so surprised?"

"I just never pictured you with a professor."

"Wait, what profession did you envision for my imaginary future beau?"

"I don't know. Maybe a reporter or an athlete trying to go pro," Lynne replied.

"And would this pretend athlete man ever make the pros?" Cassidy asked with a snort.

"I mean, I couldn't see him starting for the Steelers or anything, but maybe minor league stuff."

"You've set the bar low, haven't you?" Cassidy teased.

"Hey, I could see you with a sporty guy with big dreams," Lynne protested.

"Okay."

"I'm just saying, I was never one of those moms that was like, oh, my daughter will only marry a doctor or a lawyer."

"You didn't think I could land one, did you?" Cassidy smirked.

"I didn't say that."

"So what if I show up at dinner with a doctor or lawyer sometime?"

"I thought you liked this professor guy?"

"Ugh, I do."

"Then stop planning for the next pretend man," Lynne chuckled.

"Jake is not pretend -- he's real, and I like him a lot."

"Okay then."

"Okay," Cassidy sighed.

"Well, I'm excited to meet this not pretend professor."

"I'm glad."

"And I would be honored to be the first to meet him, so bring him straight to me when you get here," Lynne said.

Cassidy giggled. "Will do, but actually Alex already met him once."

"What?"

"We just ran into each other downtown last month," Cassidy explained.

"Alex never told me that he saw you with a boy!"

"Um, I don't know what to tell you."

"I'm going to call him and ask," Lynne said determinedly.

"You do that," Cassidy said, feeling slightly guilty that her brother was about to be scolded. But then, Alex hadn't been super warm to Jake. Maybe he deserved a light scolding.

Cassidy and Lynne chatted for another twenty minutes – most of which was Lynne updating Cassidy on her redecorating ideas for the house. After their conversation wrapped up, Cassidy hung up and called Jake to tell him the good news. He was going to meet her family!

Cassidy pulled into her parents' driveway, Jake seated in the passenger seat next to her. She shut off the engine as she looked, in slight annoyance, at all the cars already there. They had arrived early in hopes of introducing Jake to her parents privately. He was from a small family. This was going to be a long evening for him. Cassidy had hoped to ease him into the dinner – but the poor guy was about to get a crash course.

"This is where you grew up?" Jake asked, looking up at the large red brick house through the window.

"Yeah, this is home." Cassidy smiled over at him and unbuckled her seatbelt.

"When was it built?" he asked. Cassidy gave him a confused look.

"I don't know, mid-fifties? I think it was fairly new when my parents bought it. It was right after mom got pregnant with Eric and me and they needed more room."

"Oh, so--"

"Stop stalling with house questions! Time to go in. You can do this," Cassidy said encouragingly, patting his thigh.

"Yeah, yeah. It'll be great. I'm excited to meet them. They're excited to meet me."

"They are," Cassidy smiled. "I also guarantee they saw us pull into the driveway and the longer we take to get inside, the more 'making out in the car' jokes we'll get."

"Let's go!" Jake said unbuckling and hopping out of the car faster than Cassidy thought possible. She quickly followed suit and led him to the front door. She was just reaching for the door handle when it swung open. Matty stood in front of them, grinning.

"Hey kids!" Matty beamed.

"Hi! Let us in, please," Cassidy smiled.

"You're not going to introduce me?" Matty asked, feigning offense. Cassidy rolled her eyes.

"Matty, this is Jake; Jake, this is my brother, Matty."

13

Jake extended his hand, which Matty shook enthusiastically.

"So nice to finally meet you!" Matty exclaimed.

"Good to meet you, too," Jake smiled. He seemed to find Matty amusing.

"Alright, let us in," Cassidy said. Matty stepped aside and held the door open wide to let them pass.

"That's your second brother, right?" Jake asked in a low whisper. But not low enough. As Cassidy was nodding, Matty chimed in.

"Oh! Has she been preparing you? Good. 'Cause there will be a quiz at the end, and if you fail, you can't date our sister," he teased. Jake nervously chuckled.

"Ignore him. I do," Cassidy smirked. She took Jake's arm and led him into the kitchen, Matty in tow.

Lynne looked over from the island where she was chopping vegetables. She smiled as she put down the knife and wiped her hands on the pumpkin patch apron she was wearing.

"Mom, this is--"

"You must be Jacob!" she gushed.

"Jake, mom," Cassidy corrected.

"It's fine," Jake said politely as Lynne wrapped him in a hug.

"So nice to meet you!" Lynne said, looking up at him and patting his shoulders as she pulled back.

"Nice to meet you, too."

"I'm glad you could join us this evening. It's been a long time since Cassidy brought someone home for us to meet."

Cassidy bit her tongue.

"Absolute ages. We thought she'd become a nun," Matty quipped sarcastically as he leaned against the counter. Cassidy shot him a look.

Suddenly, Ben appeared in the kitchen, pushing past Matty to reach for the box of crackers behind him.

"Who's a nun?" Ben asked.

"Cassidy," Matty replied.

"I thought Alex said she was a hooker." Ben shrugged as he popped a handful of crackers in his mouth. Matty lit up.

"She can be anything she wants," Matty cooed, patting Cassidy's cheek.

"Ugh, get off me," Cassidy groaned, twitching away.

"Stop it, you three," Lynne scolded, stepping away from Jake and back to her vegetables. "You don't want to give Jake a bad first impression!"

"He's dating Cassidy; the bar's low," Ben teased. Cassidy lunged towards him, but Ben quickly scooted around Matty and out of the kitchen, causing Cassidy to ungracefully smack into Matty's shoulder.

"Ugh," Cassidy grumbled as she shook herself off and stepped away from her second brother. Matty made a show of rubbing his shoulder.

"Alright, alright," Lynne called over the scuffle. "Everyone out of my kitchen."

"Fine," Matty shrugged before departing.

"Do you need any help?" Jake offered politely, though he was still attempting to stifle his amusement.

"Thank you, Jacob."

"Jake," Cassidy interjected with a groan.

"But I've got everything set in here, so you are free to go," Lynne smiled.

"Okay." Cassidy noticed a little disappointment in his face. Clearly, he was looking for an excuse to hide out in the safety of the kitchen with Lynne as protection. The boys would never harm him in front of their mother.

"Come on," Cassidy said, grabbing his hand and giving it a squeeze. "I'll give you the tour."

"Okay."

"And don't worry, I'll protect you," she whispered in his ear playfully.

"Shut up."

Cassidy chuckled to herself as she led him out of the kitchen. They walked through the dining room into the large family room where Matty and Ben were both sprawled out on furniture while Ben flipped through channels with the remote.

"Well, you saw him briefly, but, Jake, this is Ben; Ben, this is Jake," Cassidy introduced.

"Hi," Jake said.

"Hey man," Ben said, twisting slightly on the couch to look over at him.

"What are you looking to watch?" Jake asked.

"Dunno." Ben shrugged.

"Isn't there a new episode of Miami Vice tonight?" Matty asked.

"Dunno," Ben said again.

"Is that all you can say?" Matty asked, looking slightly annoyed.

"Dunno," Ben said flatly, staring Matty in the face. Matty wasted no time in hurling a decorative pillow at his head before getting up and stomping over to him.

"You're always such an annoying little shit! Give me the remote!" Matty tried to wrestle the remote out of Ben's hands, but Ben was holding on for dear life.

"You guys make a great impression," Cassidy sighed before leading a rather amused Jake out of the room.

They went out the back door to the yard so Cassidy could show Jake where their old tree house was. She was surprised to find her dad, Alex, and Eric all seated at the large picnic table chatting and drinking beers. They all glanced over at the sound of the back storm door slamming shut behind Cassidy and Jake.

"Daughter!" Art cheered, raising his beer can to her in salute.

"Father!" she replied playfully as they walked over.

"Hi," Eric said, looking up at Jake.

"Hey! I'm Jake. You must be Eric," Jake said, holding out his hand.

"Must be?" Eric asked as they shook.

"Well, I've met Alex, and there was that whole father, daughter greeting. I met Matty and Ben inside, so by my deduction... you're Eric."

Eric watched Jake for a moment, a small smile appearing on his face.

"That was pretty funny. I'm kind of annoyed I enjoyed it so much," Eric said, looking quite amused. Jake looked positively thrilled with himself.

"You sound like your sister when I make a dumb joke she actually likes," Jake said. Both Cassidy and Eric shot him a look.

"Ooops! Lost some points there," Alex quipped as he took a sip from his can. Jake glanced at Cassidy nervously.

"Jake, this is my dad, Art; Dad, this is my boyfriend, Jake," she interjected, changing the subject.

"Hello, sir," Jake said, extending his hand. Art looked pleased with the level of respect. While Art could be playful, he was a stickler for proper behavior if the situation called

17

for it. Cassidy had previously brought home boyfriends that called him "dude," "man," and, in one unfortunate case in 11th grade, a boyfriend named Hank who would only respond with "yo!" Cassidy had actually kind of liked Hank, but when Art threatened to keep her home from junior prom if she went with him, Cassidy dumped him for her dorky lab partner in Chemistry who had been trying to woo her all year. They dated for almost two weeks. Jake was a clear improvement.

"Please, take a seat," Art said, releasing his hand and gesturing to the open spot across from him and next to Eric.

"Thank you," Jake grinned, taking his seat.

"What do you do for work?" Art asked. Cassidy smiled at Jake as she walked behind her father and took a seat next to Alex on his right.

"I work for Mercyhurst. I teach stats," Jake began. Cassidy sat back and simply soaked up the moment. The conversation flowed effortlessly between Art and Jake. Eric listened and looked fairly intrigued. As Jake was describing where Johnsonburg was off Route 6, Alex nudged her arm.

"Hey."

"Hmm?" Cassidy hummed, still looking at Jake.

"You happy?" he asked in a low voice, nudging her once more to get her full attention.

"Yeah," Cassidy said, finally looking over at him.

"Really?"

"Yes, why?" Cassidy replied, giving a confused chuckle.

Alex simply nodded. "That's what I needed to know," he said. He took a long drag from his stub of a cigarette before outting it on the wooden tabletop.

"Ew," Cassidy groaned loudly, pulling Art's attention away from Jake for the first time since they'd sat down.

"Oh, Alex," Art scolded, spotting the squashed ash residue. "Not on the table! Your mother will have a fit. Were you raised in a barn?"

"No, I was raised here." Alex rolled his eyes.

"Grange du Banquier!" Eric quipped in a French accent. Jake brought his fist to his mouth to try and hide a smile.

"Your mother is going to have a fit," Art continued, ignoring Eric's comment.

"That's why I didn't chuck it in the lawn," Alex noted. Cassidy scrunched her nose in confusion, not quite sure what point he was trying to make. Art groaned in annoyance.

"Well, I'm having your mother call you when she notices. Let you get your ass chewed out for once."

"For once?!" Alex's voice practically cracked in surprise. "I've gotten in trouble my whole life!"

"No, you haven't. That was Cassidy," Eric said smugly.

Cassidy shot him a look. "Hey! Don't hurl me under Alex's bus."

"Zero hurling occurring! Just noting that you got grounded a lot," Eric shrugged.

"Why is it my bus?" Alex asked, holding up his hands.

"The only reason you're making that notation is because Jake is sitting right here!" Cassidy said with a huff, trying to ignore how much Jake was enjoying all this.

"Not at all! It was just delightful timing," Eric smirked.

"I'm happy that worked out so nicely for you," Cassidy replied drolly.

"Alright," Art said in a warning tone. The twins nodded at each other. Truce.

Chapter 3

The five of them sat and chatted at the picnic table for another twenty minutes before Lynne poked her head out the back door and called them in for dinner. Jake once again offered to help Lynne, which she adamantly refused. However, Cassidy knew he was winning massive points with her mom. Whether that was his game plan or not, she appreciated it.

The family took their usual places at the long dining table, Art and Lynn at the head and foot. Alex, Cassidy, and Ben sat on one side, Matty and Eric on the other. Jake had been placed between Matty and Eric, and while he was seated directly across from Cassidy, she couldn't help but find his seating assignment a little mean. Nothing like tossing him in the deep end on day one.

However, Jake was able to win himself a few more bonus points with Lynne when he recited the Lutheran table prayer verbatim along with everyone else with zero hesitation.

"So, Jake," Lynne began, after all of the serving dishes had been passed around and everyone was digging into their filled plates. "What do your parents do?"

"My mom is a legal secretary and my dad was an insurance salesman," Jake replied, taking a bite of the cooked carrots.

"Oh nice. When did your dad retire?" Lynne asked curiously.

"He didn't. He passed away," Jake answered politely. The rest of the Bankers blanched in horror as Cassidy watched him and gave him a small smile. She knew this subject didn't upset him, but she still worried.

"I'm so sorry to hear that," Lynne said in a solemn voice.

"It's okay," Jake said, trying his best to give her, and everyone, a reassuring smile. "It was years ago. I'm fine, I promise."

"May I ask how he passed?" Lynne said gingerly. Jake took another forkful of carrots.

"He had a heart attack."

"Oh, wow, and he must have been young."

"He was 55. But he was constantly wined and dined, generally on red meat and cheese, and he spent most of his time in the car driving to clients or conventions. Lots of food, lots of sitting, lots of stress. It all just caught up with him," Jake answered. Cassidy so wished she was seated next to him to at least gently pat his knee under the table.

Lynne sighed pensively. Art, however, did not.

"Now, that's the way to go," he said.

"Dad!" Cassidy scolded.

"Really?" Alex asked him reproachfully. Jake looked surprised by his comment, and Matty sat anxious, waiting for a big blow up.

"Wined and dined to death on someone else's dime while doing a job I love. There are worse ways," Art pointed out.

"Oh, my God," Cassidy groaned in shock.

"Technically if you die in the middle of any dinner, it would be free," Ben noted.

"Shut up," Eric told him.

"For Pete's sake, Art!" Lynne said through gritted teeth. Alex and Eric stared at their father in horror while Matty and Ben laughed. Even Jake started to smile.

"Don't look at me like that," Art said defensively.

"Jake, I'm so sorry," Cassidy said desperately.

"It's okay, it was actually kind of funny," Jake said sheepishly as he let out a small laugh.

"You don't have to make my dad feel better," Cassidy assured him. Jake simply shrugged.

"You're kind of dark," Ben grinned.

"Yeesh," Eric said in a low voice, clearly still processing the whole unexpected interaction.

"Maybe a new topic?" Cassidy asked loudly, giving her father a final glare.

"Why are you so upset, Cassidy?"

"What?" Cassidy practically squeaked in disbelief.

"Dad!"

"Art!"

Lynne and Alex sighed in unison.

"This is going so well," Matty added sarcastically.

"I'm upset," Cassidy enunciated. "because I bring my boyfriend home to meet my family and you start dinner by cheering on his father's passing!"

"Cheering is a bit overdramatic," Art countered, resulting in a mix of groans and laughs from his wife and sons.

"Fine. When you die, I'll make sure to find someone to celebrate it. How would you feel about that?" Cassidy asked firmly.

"Honestly, depends how I go… Cancer – no way, that's too

sad, but I don't know, if I go from something spectacular like hang gliding into a jet engine or something? Then yeah, cheer me on!" Art said as he took a bite of meat. Cassidy simply stared at him.

"Where the hell did hang gliding come from?" Alex asked.

"You've literally never done or talked about doing anything adventurous," Eric pointed out.

"You think adventure is wearing the wrong-colored shirt to the golf course," Matty smirked.

"You didn't even go kayaking with my boy scout troop when I was ten," Ben added.

"I was just saying," Art began, but he was swiftly interrupted.

"You were just going to your study to get a brandy and come back when you've finished it," Lynne snapped.

"I like that idea," Art said, standing from the table.

"Aww, daddy got put in time out," Matty cooed in a baby voice. Jake looked down and stifled a laugh with a sip of his water.

"Poor bubby," Alex said with a pouted lip.

"It's not time out, you idiots," Art grumbled as he left the room, ignoring the chorus of baby talk coos from his sons.

"Ugh," Cassidy groaned loudly. "I'm so sorry, Jake."

"It's okay," Jake assured her, shaking his head in amusement.

"Ben, how's school?" Cassidy asked, desperate to establish a new topic before her father returned.

"What?" Ben asked, giving her a very confused look. Cassidy couldn't blame him; she had never once asked him about school since his first week of kindergarten.

"I'm trying, here," Cassidy nudged him.

"Oh," Ben said, finally understanding. "Um, it's fine."

"Oh, my God, school!" Eric exclaimed loudly. Cassidy gave her twin a perplexed look – as did the rest of the table.

"Yes, school. Ben goes to school," Matty enunciated slowly. Eric ignored him.

"Jake teaches at MU. Do you guys know each other?" Eric asked excitedly, gesturing back and forth between him and Ben.

"Um, I don't think so," Jake said, looking over at the youngest Banker.

"Naw. Wait, what do you teach?" Ben asked.

"Stats."

"Definitely didn't take that," Ben said.

"Yeah, my classes are never huge."

"Wait, was Carla Gearhart in your class last spring?" Ben asked.

"Yes, actually. I have her again this semester. Curly brown hair, right? Is she a friend of yours?"

"That's her!"

"Who's Carla Gearhart?" Alex asked, his mouth half full of food.

"Hot girl from my freshman dorm. We had a few classes together over the years, but she was never super social, or at least not with any of my friends. But she showed up at Scott's end of year party last May. Turns out, she failed her last stats test and came to blow off steam. Carla got shit faced and came home with me that night!" Ben beamed proudly. "So, thanks, man!" he gave Jake a playful salute.

"Benjamin!" Lynne scolded.

"Oh, um, you're welcome," Jake said warily, conflicted on how to answer.

"You're gross," Cassidy told her youngest brother flatly.

"Not gross," Ben argued.

"Be nice, Cassidy. He'd never get a date otherwise," Matty said.

"Real funny." Ben rolled his eyes.

"You have no place to talk! You were never exactly a nun," Eric said.

"Look in the mirror when you say that," Cassidy shot back.

"Ohh, ooh, no, you still have me beat on that front, dear sister," Eric grinned.

"I beat you in a lot of fronts, my twin," Cassidy gritted her teeth in annoyance. This was not how she'd wanted this evening to go.

"Alright," Lynne called loudly over the table.

"Why don't we call a truce and declare that we're all questionable people," Matty proposed.

"You guys can all be terrible; I'm practically perfection itself," Alex joked with a puffed out chest.

"How was your last cigarette?" Lynne probed in a warning tone. Alex's face fell.

"You just got roasted by mom!" Ben cheered.

"One vice!" Alex countered. Which turned out to be a very poor move, as his siblings delightedly took turns listing his shortcomings until Art returned to the dining room carrying a tumbler. He told them all to knock it off as he took to his seat.

"Do you have any siblings, Jake?" Lynne asked.

"Yes. Just one, though," Jake smiled as he took another bite.

"Sounds delightful," Ben said.

"Sounds boring," Matty noted.

"Brother? Sister? Older? Younger?" Art asked, downing the final swig of his brandy.

"Younger brother, but only by one year."

"I have one of those," Alex said, nodding at Matty. He still looked slightly irritated at Matty's recent jabs.

"And it's been magical," Matty grinned at him.

"Can you guys let him eat for a moment before further interrogation?" Cassidy asked as nicely as she could muster. Jake was never one for the spotlight. This was a lot for him.

"We're just interested in getting to know this boyfriend that you have actually brought home to meet us," Eric said with a smirk. Cassidy bit her lip.

"I got you, Cass," Ben began, tapping her forearm with the back of his hand. "Jake, did Cassidy tell you that she lost two of her teeth because she opened up the freezer door real fast and the frozen tube of orange juice fell out and hit her in the face?"

Cassidy dropped her fork loudly on her plate and leaned over with her head in her hands in shock. The rest of the table, including Jake, erupted in laughter.

"Oh my God," Cassidy groaned.

"I forgot about that!" Alex exclaimed.

"Oh, that was horrible. She looked like she was punched in the face," Lynne said.

"Essentially, I was," Cassidy said, sitting back up and looking over at her mother.

"I'm assuming these were baby teeth?" Jake asked.

"Yesss," Cassidy replied with a long, drawn-out s, trying to ignore his very entertained grin.

"She talked with a lisp for like a week after, if I remember right," Matty added.

"She did," Eric confirmed. "My second-grade teacher pulled me aside to ask what happened to her. No one could understand her! She looked so beat up."

"I didn't know that," Lynne said.

"Now Cassidy, I have to ask," Jake said seriously.

"What?" Cassidy hummed.

"Ben said you lost two teeth. Were both taken out at once, or did you get hit by a frozen orange juice tube twice?" he asked with a smirk. Cassidy gasped in surprise. She knew he could hold his own in banter, but couldn't believe he'd joined in with her brothers' ribbing so quickly. She swallowed a swear.

A chorus of cheers rang out from her brothers, all looking quite amused.

"Okay, I like him," Matty affirmed, slapping Jake on the back. Jake looked genuinely pleased.

"Ben, how do you even remember this? You were, like, a baby," Cassidy asked, turning towards him.

"I wasn't a baby. I was at least in preschool."

"We were in second grade; he would have been in preschool," Eric nodded.

"I definitely told kids," Ben admitted. Cassidy rolled her eyes.

"Well, I'm not the only one with a dumb injury. Matty broke his ankle when he jumped from the upstairs banister onto the stairs."

"I thought I might be able to fly," Matty replied flatly. "I could not." He was completely unfazed by his sister's story. Jake laughed.

"Alex got that terrible burn when he reached into the oven to get out that pie without a mitt," Art said.

"Ugh, that was a horrible Easter," Lynne sighed as she cut her food.

"Tell me about it. It was my left hand, too. I could hardly

hold a pencil for two weeks," Alex lamented as he looked at his dominant hand in front of him for a moment before picking up his fork once more and returning to his meal.

"Why did you grab a hot pie bare handed again?" Eric asked.

"It wasn't intentional. It was Easter, all the family was here, it was chaos. Mom told me to grab the pie from the oven as I was running through the kitchen. I was trying to get out of there quickly. I just didn't think," Alex admitted.

"You were in high school at that point, you should have known better," Art grumbled.

"Eighth grade," Alex corrected. "Still technically junior high."

"Splitting hairs there, boy." Art shook his head. Alex ignored him.

"What about you?" Matty asked Jake.

"What about me?"

"What stupid injuries happened in your childhood?" Alex clarified.

"Oh," Jake choked a bit on his water. He looked caught off guard.

"Come on, everyone has one," Ben prodded.

"Well…" Jake paused in thought before letting out a small chuckle. "It's not really my injury, but I was there. Well, I kind of caused it."

"You caused it?" Cassidy asked, looking thoroughly surprised. Jake shrugged.

"Oh, I have to hear this!" Eric said excitedly.

"Yeah, spill it -- um, wait, what's your last name?" Matty asked.

"Sullivan," Jake and Cassidy answered in unison.

"Spill it, Sullivan! Oh, that has a nice ring to it. I like that," Matty grinned.

"Well, when my brother, Will, and I were teenagers, we were hanging out downstairs one day. I honestly don't remember what it was about that day, but we got into a fight. It happened a lot. But we were both mad and I just.... I pushed him. And, well, I pushed much harder than I thought I did, and Will went straight back and hit the wall. Went through the wall, actually. Not the whole way, but right into the drywall." Jake said.

"Wait, what?" Cassidy gaped.

"Oh my God!"

"Shut up!"

"That's hilarious!"

"No way!"

The Banker boys reacted in a loud chorus.

"Into the drywall?" Art questioned. Jake nodded sheepishly.

"Yeah. Honestly, I felt bad. I didn't think I'd pushed him that hard," Jake admitted.

"Like, did he go through to another room or just make a dent?" Ben asked.

"Kind of in between. He went into the wall, but he was kind of just .... stuck there. I had to pull him out."

Another roar of laughter broke out around the table.

"Oh, your poor mother must've been so upset," Lynne commented as the laughs trailed off.

"Yeah, that's putting it lightly," Jake said, letting out a loud breath. Cassidy winced. Jake's mom, Claire, was a tough cookie, and definitely not someone she would like to cross.

"You got in a lot of trouble?" Ben asked.

"Yeah, my mom reamed us out for a solid twenty minutes. She wouldn't let us clean anything up as she wanted our dad to see. He was also really mad when he got home that night. I remember Will and I walking on eggshells for the next two weeks."

"Did you fix the wall?" Art asked.

"No, no, I don't think they trusted us with that. My dad fixed it a couple days later. I'm pretty sure my mom made him leave it broken that long so we couldn't forget." Jake chuckled and shook his head, playing it off.

The rest of the meal was spent swapping more stories and a fair amount of laughing. Cassidy couldn't help but smile at how seamless and easy the conversation was flowing. Most of the stories were at Cassidy's expense – when she threw up in the bus on the way to school; that time she fell off the edge of the riser at the fourth-grade spring concert at school. Even the story of the first time she got caught making out on the front porch when she was thirteen. Despite the humiliating tales, Cassidy didn't mind. The time together still felt nice. Jake fit in. Perfectly.

Chapter 4

As dinner concluded, everyone piled up their dishes and silverware to help clear the table. Cassidy hopped up to help her parents carry dishes into the kitchen. She could hear Matty start to quiz Jake on Pirates pitcher stats from their most recent dismal season.

"Cassidy," Art called as soon as they had both set their stacks next to the sink.

"Yes?"

"You like this guy?"

"Yes. Do you?" Cassidy asked, nervously biting her lip. Despite Cassidy's rebellious tendencies, she honestly did strive for her father's approval.

"He's a numbers man," Art nodded with a smile.

"Yes! Yes he is," Cassidy grinned. That was high praise from her father. Art was more vocal and exuberant with his anger than his praise, but that didn't mean he didn't give it. Small comments meant a lot coming from him, and Cassidy knew it.

Lynne appeared behind them carrying her second load of plates.

"Oh, I like him," Lynne said in an excited whisper before dropping everything in the sink with a loud clatter.

"Really?" Cassidy asked.

"Yes!" Lynne's face lit up as she turned and grabbed Cassidy's shoulders to pull her in for a hug. Cassidy's shoulders suddenly felt wet and sticky through her shirt. "Whoops," her mother chuckled, pulling back.

"Ugh, mom," Cassidy whined, frantically wiping the remnants of dinner from her sleeves.

"You'll be fine, use a dish cloth," Lynne advised as she washed her hands over top the pile of heavily used plates. Cassidy did as her mother suggested.

"I'm happy how well things are going," Cassidy commented as she dabbed at her shirt.

"You missed a spot," Art said, picking a small bit of cheese off of his daughter's other shoulder.

"Ack!" Cassidy grimaced as she quickly switched sides with the cloth.

"You're happy how well things with you and Jake are going, or how tonight is going?" Lynne asked.

"Well, both," Cassidy smiled.

"I like to hear that." Lynne smiled sweetly at her daughter.

"Thanks, mom," Cassidy said. Her heart gave a heavy thump. Both her parents' approval and a successful dinner: this night was perfect. And then Matty appeared in the opening between the dining room and kitchen.

"Cassidy? Cassidy?" He called, getting progressively louder.

"What?"

32

"Who'd you park in?"

"What?"

"Who's car did you park behind and therefore parked them in?" Matty asked in an overly enunciated tone.

"Eric, why? Who's leaving?" Cassidy asked.

"She's behind you, Eric," Matty said loudly over his shoulder.

"Matty?" Cassidy pushed.

"Matthew, who is leaving?" Art asked firmly as he closed the freezer door after retrieving a carton of ice cream.

"Put that back," Lynne scolded.

"We're just going to take Jake out for a quick spin," Matty replied simply.

"I'm sorry, what?" Cassidy asked, raising an eyebrow.

"We'll be back. Thirty minutes, an hour, tops."

"All of you?" Lynne questioned.

"Yep."

"Where are we going?" Cassidy asked as Jake and her brothers emerged from the dining room and headed to the front door.

"Oh, sorry, no, Cassidy. Boys only," Matty said as he walked into the foyer, his back to his sister.

"Jake, are you okay?" Cassidy asked in a frantic whisper, wondering what false promise or threat was making him go along with this.

Jake smiled at her before Ben pushed between them and Matty turned around to grab the front of Jake's shirt and pull him away.

"Alex," Cassidy groaned, reaching for his arm as he walked past.

"You can't come, Cassie," Alex said with a wink as

he pulled out of her grip. Cassidy turned to Eric, who was bringing up the rear of the group.

"Where the hell are you guys going?"

"Don't worry. Seriously, chill," Eric said.

"What?" Cassidy asked, stomping after him. Alex and Matty were grabbing keys while Ben was asking Jake if he knew some of his other professors.

"You boys are coming back, aren't you?" Lynne asked firmly.

"Yes," Alex answered, swapping keys with Matty.

"All of you?" Cassidy questioned. While Alex was generally pretty protective of her, and all four of them did care about her welfare, Cassidy's brothers were never the type to threaten to beat up a boyfriend. They knew Cassidy was capable and feisty enough to do it herself.

"Just go help mom," Eric smirked before turning and following the herd outside, Jake pushed along in the middle of them.

Cassidy stood on the front porch with her arms firmly crossed over her chest and watched as Alex moved his car behind hers before they all piled into Matty's Subaru. She couldn't help but wince as she watched them shove Jake into the back seat between Ben and Alex. Matty honked twice before they departed the driveway at a concerning speed. Eric grinned at her from the front seat. Cassidy swore under her breath before returning inside the house.

"Want a brandy?" Art asked calmly as he stood in the foyer eating vanilla ice cream out of the carton with a spoon.

"I thought mom took that from you," Cassidy said with a raised eyebrow.

"You better not rat me out." Art winked at her before

walking past her to his study. Cassidy smiled as he pushed his door closed and she went to the kitchen.

"Cassidy, have you seen your father? Did he go with the boys?" Lynne asked.

"He wasn't in the car with them," Cassidy replied honestly.

"Oh, he doesn't help anyway," Lynne sighed.

"Here, let me." Cassidy pushed up her sleeves and reached into the sink. She knew keeping busy would be best for her, but she also felt bad for her mom being deserted after dinner.

"I think this is a good thing," Lynne said after a couple minutes of washing and drying in silence.

"Really?"

"Yes! I don't remember your brothers ever wanting to spend time with one of your boyfriends before.... Or at least not all four of them," Lynne mused as she dried another plate.

"Thus making it more concerning. This feels like a plot to take him out to the country where an accident occurs and they bury him in a field," Cassidy said, adding more dish soap to the sponge.

"I couldn't see that. None of them are good at digging," Lynne joked, giving a side eye to her daughter. Cassidy froze and took a deep breath to avoid spitting out something she would regret.

"Ha-ha, mom," she said drolly.

"I thought it was pretty good," Lynne said with a proud smile.

"It's just weird."

"I mean… it's new. But seems like they want to be friends."

"Friends?"

"Yes! Or they just want to make fun of you without you in earshot," Lynne said.

"No, they prefer to mock me in person."

"Well, then they're hanging out with their new friend." Lynne shrugged.

"Fine," Cassidy said with a sigh. She didn't feel like arguing with her mother, or allowing herself to spiral as she thought about all the depraved possibilities.

Lynne seemed to understand and began to regale Cassidy with the drama of their neighbor's botched landscaping project and all the troubles their multiple fixes had caused. Cassidy enjoyed the distraction, as well as the story. Once they had finished cleaning up, they helped themselves to the apple pie Lynne had made and settled in the family room.

Art appeared twenty minutes later to join them. Unfortunately, he openly carried the now empty tub of ice cream to throw out and got an earful from Lynne. Despite valiant attempts on her father's part, Lynne denied him a slice of pie. Art grumbled to himself as he took a seat on the couch next to his daughter.

"Was it good?" he asked, pointing at her empty plate on the coffee table.

"Delicious," Cassidy winked. Art gave a pathetic sigh that made Cassidy giggle. The three of them watched TV in a comfortable silence for awhile until they were interrupted by the sound of the front door banging open, startling them all.

"Oh, for Pete's sake," Art grumbled as he clumsily folded his newspaper in annoyance.

"We're back!" Matty's voice rang out from the foyer. Lynne and Cassidy shared a look before hopping to their feet.

"All of you?" Cassidy asked pointedly as she walked through the dining room and into the kitchen where Matty was opening the fridge in search of a snack.

"Think so," Matty replied sarcastically. Cassidy turned to see her other brothers and Jake coming through the foyer into the kitchen. All looked surprisingly jovial. Without hesitation, Cassidy made a beeline for Jake and hugged him.

"Hi," Jake chuckled, surprised by her intensity.

"I didn't get a hug," Alex noted as he walked past the two.

"Shut up," Cassidy said as she pulled back from Jake.

"Rude!" Ben added. Cassidy ignored him.

"Are you okay?"

"Yeah, great," Jake smiled.

"Really?"

"Jeez, she really doesn't trust us," Matty said, pulling the pie out of the fridge and placed it on the island.

"Nope," Ben said, waiting plate in hand for the pie.

"Sad, really," Eric smirked. Cassidy rolled her eyes.

"Wait, wait, wait," Lynne called. She rushed into the room and intercepted the knife in Matty's hands.

"Mom?"

"I love that she still doesn't trust you with sharp knives," Alex teased.

"I trust him with a knife," Lynne sighed, slicing the pie herself, "But I don't trust the size and shape that these pieces will come out."

Matty attempted to argue his abilities as everyone tossed in jabs. Lynne dished out perfect pieces of pie to her four sons and Jake. Art once again attempted to get a slice but was swiftly rebuffed by Lynne, much to his children's amusement.

They all settled in the family room as the boys enjoyed dessert and Lynne asked Jake a lot of questions about his time at Penn State. Art even managed to convince Eric to give him the final bite of his pie when Lynne was distracted.

Chapter 5

They were less than ten minutes from the Banker family home. Cassidy was just merging onto the interstate to head north and, other than commenting on the pie, Jake hadn't said a word. She was ready to get the full story now that they were way out of earshot of the family.

"Soooo," Cassidy hummed loudly as she turned the radio volume down low.

"What?" Jake asked, as if popping out of a daze.

"Don't play dumb, you know exactly what I'm asking."

"Oh, yes! Your parents are great!" Jake smiled.

"Jake," Cassidy whined, giving him a playful swat. "Where did you guys go? What did you do? I haven't seen any obvious bleeding."

"The blood oath is next visit," Jake said with a smirk. Cassidy held back a laugh.

"You're seriously not going to tell me? You only met them today!"

"No, duh… I'm kidding."

"We still have thirty minutes in this car together," Cassidy pointed out as she merged lanes to pass a slow-moving minivan. "Were you sworn to secrecy or something?"

"No, no. They knew I couldn't keep my mouth shut with you without getting hit," Jake chuckled.

"Come on, then! Please?" Cassidy asked sweetly.

"It was less exciting than you think. We just all got in Matty's car--"

"I saw that part."

"Yeah, and we just took these country roads – honestly there were a few moments I thought I might be killed. There were just fields around us. But a few minutes later we ended up at this lake."

"Lake? Tamarack Lake?" Cassidy asked.

"Dunno, maybe."

"If it was only a few minutes and all back roads, probably."

"But they just pulled onto the grass, and we got out. Matty opened the trunk and there was a case of beer. We just had a drink, hung out, skipped rocks on the water. It was nice," Jake explained.

Cassidy felt very confused. "What?"

"Yeah! It was nice."

"Nice?!"

"You didn't think it would be?"

"Obviously not," Cassidy said, smacking her palm on the steering wheel.

"You're upset I didn't get my ass kicked?" Jake chortled.

"No, no. I'm just … confused."

"You're confused?"

"I mean, like, they've never done that before. They've never taken my boyfriends out for beers. Not even the one I dated for two years. And they just met you today and you're already hanging out with them."

"Wait, are you mad?"

"No! No, definitely not. I just was surprised they coordinated all this."

"I mean, no one is more surprised than me, but they did tell me they had this plan to leave if they hated me. They were just going to get up and go and leave us with your parents – which of course would have been fine -- but they liked me, kind of, and so I got to join."

"Liked you?" Cassidy asked.

"I think Ben's exact words were that I wasn't the 'dipstick loser' he expected." Jake grinned proudly. Cassidy couldn't help but laugh.

"That's quite a compliment coming from him."

"I felt like it was," Jake chuckled.

"So, they were just planning on escaping?"

"But apparently I didn't suck, so I got to tag along,"

"No, you don't suck," Cassidy said with a smile, leaning over to her right slightly. Jake took the hint and kissed her on the cheek. They rode in a comfortable silence for a few minutes. The sounds of Huey Lewis and Peter Frampton on the radio filled the car before Jake spoke again.

"They really love you."

"Hmm?" Cassidy asked, her focus on the cars merging from the on-ramp into her lane.

"Your family," Jake clarified.

"Oh, I know, and I love them. Even when they drive me crazy," Cassidy smiled.

"More than that. Just the way your brothers talked about you when it was just us…"

"Oh jeez, what stories did they tell you?"

"None."

"None?"

"No, not like when we were at the table. They wanted your reaction there."

"Ugh, I still can't believe they brought up half of those things." Cassidy shook her head.

"Yeah," Jake chuckled. "Like, they make the jokes, but they want you to be happy more than anything. And I know that I'm only in their good graces if you're happy."

"They're not beat you up type guys."

"Well," Jake winced. "I was actually given explicit warnings. And frankly, I believe they would follow through."

"Which one said it?"

"Kind of a group consensus."

"Jake, just remember: Alex is a pacifist, Matty is a joker, Eric is super aloof, and Ben, well, honestly, Ben may give it a hearty try, but he'd lose interest quickly," Cassidy said.

"Don't shrug them off. They'd do more for you than you give them credit for," Jake said seriously. Cassidy's heart gave a thump. She wanted to make a joke, but she couldn't. The truth was, she knew her brothers loved her. But tonight, as they took Jake under their wing, she had full proof of their respect for her. If she were alone in the car, she would cry. Tears of joy, tears of gratitude, tears of love.

"I won't," Cassidy said quietly after a long pause. Jake gave her knee a firm squeeze before changing the subject to the Steelers game coming up on Sunday. They passed the rest of the car ride happily chit chatting about sports, TV, and food. The time flew by and before they knew it, they were back in Cassidy's apartment parking lot.

41

"Do you want to come upstairs?" Cassidy asked, as she removed the keys from the ignition.

"I can't stay over, but I can come up for a little bit," Jake said.

"Why can't you stay over tonight?"

"Because I'm exhausted, but also, my shoes and jeans have lake water and mud on them and I really want to change. I don't want to put these back on tomorrow," Jake admitted. Cassidy grinned.

"That's very understandable," she said before leaning forward and kissing him. Jake kissed her back.

"Thank you for introducing me to your family," Jake said.

"I'm really glad you came; it meant a lot," Cassidy told him honestly, as she rested her forehead against him. "I'm just so happy that it went so well."

"Me too." Jake kissed her once more.

"I love you," Cassidy whispered.

"I love you, too."

"Are you sureeeee you can't stay over?" Cassidy asked playfully, though she knew and understood the answer.

"No," he chuckled. "But what are you doing tomorrow?"

"Marissa and I are going grocery shopping, and I'd like to go for a run, but otherwise I'm free."

"Can I come over and join you for--"

"A run?" Cassidy asked, absolutely shocked.

"Well, I started to ask that, but then I realized how embarrassing it would be."

"I'd go slow for you," Cassidy winked as she ran her thumb over the stubble on his cheek. Damn, she wanted him.

"Oh! I meant embarrassing for you," Jake quipped proudly. Cassidy pushed his chest hard and tried not to laugh, but failed miserably.

"Shut up!"

"No, seriously, running sounds horrible, but I'd love to see you after."

"I could use a shower buddy."

"Now that, I could do," Jake grinned before kissing her once more.

"How did it go, guys?" Marissa's voice rang through the apartment as soon as Cassidy entered.

"Just me," Cassidy replied as she locked the door and dropped her purse and keys in the entry.

"Just you? Uh oh," Marissa grimaced as she sat up on the couch. Cassidy took a seat at the opposite end.

"No, no, no need to worry," Cassidy said, slipping off her shoes and propping her feet up on the coffee table.

"Soooooo, how did it go?"

"Honestly, really well."

"Yeah?" Marissa smiled.

"Everyone got along well! I mean, most of the stories my brothers told were at my expense…"

"Obviously."

"But in the weirdest turn of events ever, the boys took Jake out for a beer."

"Wait, what?" Marissa asked, sitting up slightly.

"Yeah. Apparently the guys had a whole thing planned to escape if they hated Jake, but they ended up taking him with them."

"But Jake's not here now?"

"No."

"Is he dead?"

"No, he's not dead! He rode home in the car with me." Cassidy shook her head.

"Hmmm."

"What?"

"Maybe he's got head trauma?"

"He didn't look or act hurt. He said he had fun – he even defended them! He was wet and dirty from the lake and he wanted to change. I get it. He doesn't have any clothes here."

"Hmm," Marissa hummed once more. She looked as if she was in deep thought.

"Spit it out, Solomon."

"Look, I love your family, but I can only imagine how intimidating it was for Jake."

"Yeah, he was nervous on the way over. But he was having fun and laughing pretty quickly – mostly at embarrassing stories of me, but still."

"Fair." Marissa shrugged. "I'm just wondering if Jake would actually tell you if something did happen?"

Cassidy made a face as she pondered for a moment.

"Well, I'm seeing him tomorrow. I can ask him then."

"Oh, you mean when he comes over to have sex with his hot girlfriend while she has the apartment to herself?"

"It's shower sex I promised him, actually," Cassidy winked. Marissa rolled her eyes.

"Well yeah, I'm sure he'll be real honest then. Guys are known for their honesty before sex."

"Well, I'll ask him after, then," Cassidy sighed.

"Mmmhmm,"

"Maybe not. Maybe I don't care what really happened and

am happy to believe his lie?"

"Then you're lying to yourself. I know you, Cassidy. You have to know everything!" Marissa smirked at her.

"Dammit!" Cassidy groaned playfully before chucking a decorative pillow at Marissa's head, making her laugh.

"Can I just ask you one favor, in regard to Jake?" Marissa asked after a long moment.

"What's that?"

"Can you please bleach the friggin' shower and tub before I get back on Sunday afternoon?

Cassidy snorted. "Deal."

Chapter 6

Cassidy bounded up the stairs of her apartment building, taking them two at a time. She had just finished a three mile run in under twenty five minutes. She was feeling very pleased with herself as she exited the stairwell and pulled out her key to let herself into her apartment. Marissa had been packing up for an overnight at her boyfriend Brandon's when she was departing for her run, so they had already said their goodbyes. As much as Cassidy loved coming home to her best friend, and they were both comfortable when the other had a guy over for the night, she kind of enjoyed the opportunity to have the place to herself for a few hours.

"Record time!"

Cassidy jumped slightly. She was not expecting anyone to be home, let alone hearing a male voice. She grabbed one of the long umbrellas that was resting against the wall by the door. She was ready to attack.

"Hello?" Cassidy raised the umbrella to her shoulder like a bat.

"Hey Cass-! Whoa!" Jake popped out of the living room into the hall, but stumbled back a few feet at the sight of his weapon-wielding girlfriend.

"Jake?" Cassidy dropped the umbrella with a thud. "You scared the hell out of me!"

"Sorry," Jake held his hands up in surrender, although he appeared more amused than remorseful.

"How did you get in?" Cassidy walked over and placed a light kiss on his lips.

"Marissa let me in."

"Oh."

"You called me when you were leaving for your run, so I just came right over. Glad I did, I only got here about five minutes ago and Marissa was just heading out the door. I think I scared her, too."

"You're doing great today," Cassidy teased.

"I try."

"I'm glad you're here."

"How was your run?"

"Great! Made good time."

"Ready for a cool down?" Jake asked with a smirk, gently playing with the fabric on the sides of her t-shirt. Cassidy couldn't help but grin.

"Or a warm up?"

"Yes, either or," Jake said. Cassidy gave his chest a light push and took a step back. She slipped off her sneakers and pulled her tee over her head, tossing it on the back of the sofa before turning to walk toward the bathroom.

"Coming?" she asked. She could hear Jake scrambling behind her and the thump of his shoes as she flipped on the bathroom light.

47

Jake's hands were on her hips by the time she crossed the threshold. She grinned, her back towards him. He spun her around so that she faced him. He had already removed his shirt. Cassidy pushed herself up on her toes and connected her lips to his in a kiss that deepened on impact. Jake's right hand cupped her butt tightly, making her heart flutter. She roughly pushed him back after a long minute. He looked a mix of shocked and concerned, but Cassidy gave him a reassuring wink and bent down to pull off her socks, which she had to admit were disgusting. She quickly balled them up and threw them back into the hall over Jake's shoulder.

"Close the door," Cassidy instructed. He kicked it closed behind him. She smirked at him as she pulled her sports bra over her head, leaving her in her dark green running shorts. She pulled back the floral shower curtain and started the water. Jake reached over and traced her bare back as she checked the water temperature. Cassidy bit her lip at the gentle touch.

"The freckles on your back look like constellations," he smiled.

"I think that's a compliment," Cassidy giggled as he continued to trace her back.

"It is," he hummed. Cassidy flipped the lever on the tap and the water streamed from the shower head. She turned and grinned at him before looping her thumbs in the waistband of her shorts and panties and pushing them to the floor. She stepped into the shower completely naked.

"Joining me?"

"It's quite a view," Jake breathed, taking her in.

"Pants off," Cassidy said, closing the curtain behind her and letting the warm water pour over her sweaty body. She had less than thirty seconds to herself before the curtain pulled back and Jake stepped in behind her. He wasted no time, placing his hand on her stomach and pulling her back against his naked body. Cassidy gasped at the feeling of all of his skin on all of her. She loved it.

Jake held her tightly with his left hand as his right slowly ran up and down her torso in an almost rhythmic fashion. From her neck, to her breasts, down her stomach, to the junction of her legs and back up. Repeating over and over as the water beat down on them. Within a minute, Cassidy's breathing was shaky, and had no chance to steady as Jake's lips suddenly attached to her neck.

Cassidy felt her legs go weak. Her body was on fire, especially now that Jake's erection was firmly pushing into her hip. She turned around to face him and grabbed the back of his head with her hands and crashed her lips onto his. She needed to taste him. The kiss deepened. Cassidy kept one hand on his head, her fingers entwined in his hair, while bringing the other to his back, practically clawing at him to hold on.

Jake wrapped his left arm around her middle, as his right went to her ass, gripping tightly and lifting her up slightly so she was on her tip toes. Cassidy was soaring. She tried to remind herself to breathe, but it was becoming more difficult between the water showering over them, and Jake's mouth moving in sync with hers.

They kissed for a long minute, then suddenly Jake picked her up and firmly pushed her back against the wall under the shower head. She clipped the edge of her back on the shower dial, causing her to grunt in pain.

"Ugh!"

"What?" Jake asked as the water hit his face.

"Dial."

"Shit."

"Other side," Cassidy instructed, pointing over his shoulder. Jake didn't need any more instruction. He quickly spun them around and pushed her the few feet to the back of the tub and up against the wall.

A weird hot/cold feeling came over her. Jake's back was blocking all the water and the cool tile was pressed against her back – but the heat between her and Jake was radiating.

They stared at each other for a long second, breathing heavily. And then Jake's mouth captured hers once more. Cassidy gripped his upper back tightly with her right arm as her left reached up to grab the metal bar the shower curtain hung from. She prayed it was as sturdy as she thought.

Jake used his knee to push her legs apart. His firm need for her was pushing at the junction of her legs, making Cassidy shiver. She propped one of her feet up on the edge of the tub. Jake kissed her hard as he entered her. Cassidy gasped into his mouth as he pressed her harder against the shower wall.

It took them a few moments to get a rhythm going at that angle, and Cassidy clawed at Jake's back – she was pretty sure there was going to be a deep scratch. But her mind was absorbed in the wild sensations shooting through her.

Their kisses quickly became gasps. Cassidy's eyes locked on the shower head over Jake's shoulder; it was almost hypnotic to focus on it. She no longer felt any cold from the tile. Only heat. Sparks radiating through to her extremities. Time no longer made sense and for a few moments she actually thought she was floating. The feelings were building in her and her head tilted up to let out a cry as she climaxed. Jake kissed her and pushed her even harder against the tile, holding her firmly in place. Cassidy wondered how she wasn't going through the wall. He pulled out of her and let out a loud cry, spilling on the tile next to her thigh. Cassidy gasped again in gratification.

Slowly he loosened his grip on her and she let go of the shower bar – which had held its own quite nicely -- and lowered her feet to the tub floor.

Jake cupped her face and kissed her slowly, pulling her back under the warm water.

"Oh, my God," Jake sighed in a low voice. He smiled at her with the water dripping down his face.

"Oh, my God," Cassidy repeated, grinning up at him. They enjoyed a quiet moment where they didn't talk, they didn't think, they just held each other under the water and enjoyed the intimate closeness.

After a few minutes Cassidy kicked Jake out of the shower so she could actually get clean. He laughed as he exited the tub to dry off, re-dress, and return to lounging in the living room while Cassidy finished.

Five minutes later, she emerged from the steamy bathroom wrapped in a fluffy pink towel. She smiled at Jake, who was stretched out on the couch reading a magazine, his hair still damp and slightly disheveled. Her heart gave a thump at the sight of him. She loved him so much.

"Hey," he said, looking over at her. She could tell he was thinking the same thing she was.

"Hi."

"What are you doing?"

"I'm going to go to my room and get dressed."

"Can I come?" he asked. Cassidy gave a small laugh and paused a moment to consider it.

"Not this time. I'll be out in a few minutes."

"Okay."

"Okay," she smiled before going turning into her room and shutting the door. She couldn't stop smiling. How was this so perfect? Cassidy padded over to her closet and slid the door open. She looked at her wardrobe, trying to decide what to wear. She dropped the towel on the floor as she reached to grab a hanger. Cassidy paused and glanced over at her reflection in the full length mirror on the back of her door. She couldn't lie. She looked good.

"Fuck it," she said with a sigh as she returned the hanger to the rail and went to open her bedroom door.

"Jake!" Cassidy yelled, standing completely naked in the door frame. Jake popped up.

"What? -oh!" He looked pleasantly surprised.

"Get your ass in here," Cassidy said, nodding towards her room. Jake didn't hesitate for a moment. He leapt up, hurdled over the back of the couch and wrapped his arms around Cassidy. She giggled as he tackled her to the bed. They were ready for round two.

Chapter 7

Cassidy picked up one of the small red and white bows from the large pile next to her and attached it to the top center of the 5x7 card in front of her. She was currently sitting in an assembly line on the floor of Ellie's parents' large living room helping put together wedding bulletins.

Eric's fiancé, Ellie Hammond, had reached out to her the previous week and invited her to a wedding prep evening at her parents'. Cassidy happily accepted, however the joy was waning a bit as she was forty-five minutes into ribbon gluing, which was preceded by dinner placement card writing, paper flower making, and a short-lived glitter sprinkling session. Unfortunately, while passing the glitter container down the line, there was an inexplicable, but very quick succession of slippery fingers, fumbling, attempted recovery, and finally a drop, which ended in what Cassidy could only describe as a glitter explosion. This resulted in a grievous ten minutes of vacuuming and sweeping: a low point in the evening for all involved. Though, most notably, for the Hammond family's tabby cat, Bonkers, who rolled in some of the displaced glitter before running away from the many hands trying to catch him. Bonkers retreated to the top of the stairs, where he tried to clean the sparkle off of himself, and then shortly after vomited, rather festively, on the kitchen floor. Cassidy felt for Bonkers. He was immediately whisked upstairs to the bathroom for a glitter removing bath by Ellie's mom, May, and then force-fed some medicine. He was currently on his third round of cleaning his still damp fur on the small throw rug in front of the fireplace next to Cassidy.

Cassidy decided that Bonkers was a kindred spirit. She was as over tonight's festivities as he was. She appreciated the camaraderie, even in feline form.

"Hey, last one!" Molly called out happily, waving a final invitation in the air. They all sighed with relief. While there were seven of them there, the work had been a slog. Ellie's older sister Kara was her maid of honor. Molly, Lisa, Elaine, and Mindy, her other four bridesmaids, were also there. While all of them were nice and friendly enough -- aside from Kara, who Cassidy found to be super bossy and a bit of a pill -- she knew they wouldn't leave the evening as best friends. Cassidy felt like the outsider, a feeling she was not used to, nor did she enjoy.

Once all the bulletins were prepped, pretty, and settled in a large plastic storage box for safe keeping, the girls stood up and stretched.

"Ellie, what else do we need to help with?" Elaine asked, picking a few remaining bits of glitter off of her arm.

"I think we did everything. Thank you guys so much!" Ellie grinned. Cassidy tried not to look too relieved.

"Glad we could help; this was fun!" Elaine gushed. Suddenly the room was filled with squeals and thank yous and hugs. Cassidy managed to dodge most of it, but Molly and Lisa both snagged an embrace. They all grabbed coats and purses and made their way to the front door.

"Mimosas at Shanty's next weekend?" Mindy asked the group. A chorus of yeses filled the small foyer.

"Cassidy, are you going to join us? You should!" Molly said, catching Cassidy completely off guard.

"Oh, oh, um, maybe. I need to check my book, but thank you!" Cassidy smiled.

"Good!" Elaine grinned. Cassidy was the back of the line as they filed outside. Before she crossed the threshold, Ellie caught her arm.

"Cass, you wanna stay?" she asked in a whisper.

"Oh, um, yeah," Cassidy replied with a shrug. She had no other plans that evening, and frankly avoiding the lengthy driveway chit-chat was much appreciated. Ellie closed the door behind her friends and held out her arms to take Cassidy's coat once more. They returned to the large living room where Kara and May were finishing tidying up.

"Cassidy?" Kara asked, looking surprised to see her.

"Hey!"

"I asked her to hang out for a bit – we are going to be related soon," Ellie said walking over to the large brown and tan couch and taking a seat. Cassidy followed suit.

"You look like your brother, you know," Kara commented.

"Yeah, we're twins."

"I know," Kara replied blandly. Cassidy withheld an eye roll.

"I'm glad that Ellie is going to have a sister in that family with all of those brothers." May smiled at her. She was a petite woman with long silky black hair down the middle of her back and a brown and teal headband pushing her hair out of her tanned face. Cassidy liked her a lot. She could see the joy in her face helping her daughter with her wedding. Cassidy could only imagine Lynne would love her, as well.

"Happy to be there to run defense. Maybe toughen her up a bit," Cassidy winked.

"Wax on, wax off," Ellie said with a smirk. Cassidy appreciated the movie reference and grinned at her.

"Yes, Ellie-san."

"Well, I think she's pretty tough as she is," Kara challenged. Cassidy focused hard to keep her face neutral.

"Very true."

"Cassidy, would you like some tea?" May offered.

"I'd love some, thank you, Mrs. Hammond."

"May, please! Girls?"

"Yes, please," Ellie said.

"No thanks, I'm going to go. Max said he'd take me out for drinks tonight and I want to get cleaned up," Kara responded, flipping her hair dramatically before departing. May followed her out, asking her questions about dinner the next day. Cassidy let out a low breath of relief at Kara's departure.

"You didn't say anything," Ellie said.

"Hmm?"

"With Kara, you didn't say anything. You're usually the one of the group with the best comebacks! Well, you and Matty."

"I'm honored."

"But not a word?"

"I'm a guest. I don't make sassy comments as a guest. I'm not a neanderthal!"

"You disappoint me, Banker," Ellie smirked.

Cassidy was amused. "Oh, I like you."

"Yes!" Ellie cheered playfully, pumping her fist in celebration. Cassidy laughed.

"It's fun to see you away from my brother. You're... different."

"Different?"

"Well, more relaxed, maybe?"

"I'm quite relaxed with Eric. It's just at big events... Your family is nice, but you guys kind of scare the crap out of me sometimes," Ellie admitted.

"Not the first time I've heard that."

"Really?"

"Oh yeah."

"It's getting better," Ellie said.

"I hope it does," Cassidy said honestly. The sound of the front door closing rang through the house and May appeared in the kitchen once more.

"I'm boiling the water!" she called out.

"Thanks, mom."

"Hey, I haven't seen your dad. Is he here?" Cassidy asked.

"He's at work."

"Saturday at 8PM? What does he do?"

"He's a paramedic."

"On an ambulance?"

"Yeah."

"That's really cool!"

"It is. He loves it. But the hours always suck."

"Yeah, I bet. Emergencies aren't really nine-to-five."

"Nope. He's on for forty-eight hours, off for forty-eight hours."

"Ugh," Cassidy grimaced.

"Yeah."

Suddenly a little chirp of a meow caught their attention. Bonkers had hopped up on the couch next to Cassidy.

"Hello," Cassidy smiled at the almost fully dry tabby.

"Wow," Ellie said, watching Cassidy hold up her hand for Bonkers to sniff before he leaned forward slightly, wanting pets. Cassidy happily obliged.

"Hmm?"

"He doesn't usually take to new people so quickly."

"Maybe he thinks I'm Eric," Cassidy said as she scratched Bonkers behind the ears.

"No, he doesn't really like Eric," Ellie snorted. Cassidy beamed.

"What a good kitty," she said in a playful voice.

"I'm surprised you like him."

"What's not to like? He's cute, he's friendly, he has great taste in people."

"I just thought you were a dog person."

"I like all animals! Well, not slugs, they're gross, but animals in general? I'm a big fan."

"Good to know. Eric has talked about the dogs you guys had."

"We've had two dogs. Oscar, who was a chocolate lab that my parents got while they were dating. He was nice, but he passed when I was four. And then the next year we got our dalmatian, Domino." Cassidy rolled her eyes. "He was dumber than a box of hair. I love dogs, but I'm shocked Domino didn't put me off."

"Poor Domino," Ellie chuckled.

"Don't feel sorry for him. He was a mess. And after he

passed, my mom was very adamant on not having any more animals," Cassidy explained. Bonkers, who was now purring loudly, settled down and sat his front half on her lap while his back feet remained on the couch.

"Remarkable," Ellie commented. Cassidy smiled proudly.

Cassidy and Ellie talked about work until May came over with their hot tea cups and joined them in the living room. She had a long list of questions for Cassidy. They all shared stories of childhood and school. They laughed at favorite movie quotes and talked about their favorite holiday recipes. Before Cassidy realized it, it was almost 9:30. She truly enjoyed her time with Ellie and her mom and saw why Eric loved her. After dislodging a sleeping Bonkers, she helped take dishes to the sink before, once again, putting on her coat and slinging her purse over her shoulder.

"Thank you for letting me stay, this was great," Cassidy told Ellie honestly. Ellie launched forward and hugged her tightly, surprising Cassidy a bit. She hugged her back.

"It was nice to meet you," May said, gently squeezing her shoulders.

"Thank you for the tea, and remind me once more, when are you meeting my parents?"

"Is it in two weeks?" May looked at Ellie.

"Yes, you and dad are coming to Erie and we're all having dinner at that Italian place by Eric's house," Ellie told her mom. Cassidy reached over and held onto her arm gently.

"Promise that you'll use the payphone in the lobby and call me if you need back up. I can be there in ten minutes," Cassidy winked. May let out a loud laugh.

"I will keep that in mind."

After a final goodbye, Cassidy stepped outside into the

dark and cold. It was mid-October, and in northwestern Pennsylvania, that meant snow could show up anytime from now until April. She shivered as she walked to the large, dirt driveway where her car sat. It smelled like snow. The Hammonds lived in the country on a four acre plot. It was beautiful in the daytime, but felt creepy at night. Cassidy missed the lights of the city. She was unlocking her car door when she was met with very bright lights – two car lights ambling towards her and parking to the right of her car.

"You're here?" Eric said, hopping out of his car.

"Yes, I was helping with wedding things." Cassidy smiled at her twin.

"I know, I'm just surprised you're still here," he said, rounding the car to come stand next to her.

"I was invited to stay after the others left. I really like Ellie!"

"Really?"

"Yes, really! I had a wonderful time."

"I didn't know how you'd get along with her friends."

"Oh, well, that part was just okay. Her friends are nice. Her sister is a bit of a pill."

"Hmmm," Eric hummed, which Cassidy knew meant he agreed, but would never say it so he had deniability.

"And her mother is so sweet!"

"She is. Both of her parents are really nice."

"Oh, hey," Cassidy swatted his arm. "I heard there's a parents dinner coming up. Can I please get an invite?"

"Absolutely not!"

"Ugh, but can you at least tell me everything that's said afterwards?" Cassidy asked. Eric rolled his eyes.

"I'll only tell you if mom or dad put their foot in their mouth."

"That's literally all I care about hearing!" Cassidy grinned childishly.

"Go home, Cassidy."

"Wait, why are you out here so late?"

"I'm picking up Ellie. Her friend Molly had driven her out here and I promised I'd bring her home after she had some time with her mom."

"Well aren't you the knight in shining armor," Cassidy teased.

"Yes. Yes, I am. Now go home."

"I will, and I will call Matty to let him know that we're going to have fantastic Lynne and Art out in public stories coming soon!"

"God, you're annoying."

"Drive safe, little brother."

"We're twins."

"I'm twelve minutes older than you."

"You did nothing in that time."

"How would you know? You weren't even there." Cassidy smirked as she opened her car door.

"Good night, Cassidy," Eric said, walking toward the house.

"Hey, Eric!"

"What?" Eric asked, turning around.

"Bonkers sat on my lap and purred," she said smugly.

"What?"

"It was high quality cat time."

"The last time I was here and went to pet him, he swatted me and nicked my hand with his claw."

"Best. Cat. Ever." Cassidy said as Eric groaned.

"Stupid cat."

"Be nice. Bonkers is my friend!" Cassidy yelled, then

hopped inside her car and closed the door. Eric flipped her off as she let her car idle a moment to warm up.

Cassidy smiled the whole way home.

Chapter 8

December 1987

It had been a fairly uneventful month and a half for Cassidy. She and Jake were spending a few nights a week together. Over the Halloween weekend, she, Jake, Marissa, and Brandon went to a huge Halloween party at Edinboro University for the alumni. It was the best party Cassidy had been to in years. Both she and Marissa enjoyed showing the boys around their old haunts.

All four of them spent Thanksgiving with their respective families. Both Ellie and Laura joined the Bankers for their holiday meal. Alex's 29th birthday was the following day, so a combination Thanksgiving and birthday meal made for a fun and food-filled day. Given the celebratory nature of the event, only two arguments managed to break out and a single dish was broken: a holiday record for the Bankers!

Work had gone from a nice constant in Cassidy's life to a stressful and depressing daily trudge. Since Devon's firing, her office had seen three other accountants, two more office staff, and all perks - from coffee to heating - removed from the building. The fact that Cassidy remained was no longer a blessing, but a curse. Between long hours, extra reports, angry clients, general office discomfort, and the hateful glares from her remaining coworkers, all wondering when their number would be up, Cassidy was considering quitting. Both Jake and Marissa told her to look for a new job on a daily basis. While Cassidy knew they were right, she also knew that if she stuck it out to the end, and took on every crummy task Mr. Jelif assigned, he would write her a hell of a recommendation. She wanted that letter. She needed it.

It was Friday, December 4th - the first Friday of the month and her family's monthly dinner gathering. Despite seeing everyone the previous week for Thanksgiving, Cassidy was really looking forward to it. They were also celebrating Matty's 28th birthday, which had been on Wednesday. That meant ice cream cake, Matty's favorite dessert -- one he always fought for, arguing it wasn't fair he never got it, just because he had a winter birthday. Cassidy couldn't lie. He had a point.

The thought of a good, home cooked meal followed by ice cream cake was getting Cassidy through the week. She was currently eating her fifth packed turkey sandwich of the week as she opened another client folder and worked through lunch once again.

"Banker!" The familiar voice of her boss, Mr. Jelif, made her head snap up.

"Yes?"

"Oh," he noticed she was holding half of a sandwich in her left hand. "Um, finish up your lunch, then come to my office, please."

"I can come now."

"No, no, please, eat and wrap up what you're working on," Mr. Jelif gave a weak smile and nod before weaving his way through the bullpen and back to his office. Cassidy let out a low sigh, not looking forward to finding out what additional work she was about to be assigned.

Less than fifteen minutes later, Cassidy had eaten her sandwich and managed to balance the budget proposal for one of the clients she'd inherited. She closed and placed the file in her outbox, straightened her black skirt, and made her way to Mr. Jelif's office.

"Come in," he called at the sound of her knock.

"You asked for me?" Cassidy asked with a smile.

"Yeah, come in and close the door."

"What's up?" she asked, taking a seat in the chair across from him. At this point, the chair was downright familiar.

"Banker, I'm sorry," Mr. Jelif said with a sigh.

"Hmmm?"

"You've worked very hard and it's been appreciated."

"That sounds like I'm getting fired," Cassidy said lightly. Mr. Jelif looked uncomfortable.

"Oh."

"Banker... Cassidy..."

"Wh-wh-what does this mean?"

"It means you will not be working here anymore," he said. Cassidy bit the inside of her cheek to keep from swiping back with a sassy reply.

"No, I... I know what fired means, but is everyone done?"

"Um, well..."

"So, no."

"You don't need to be concerned anymore."

"Oh." Cassidy swallowed hard.

"I hope you know this is not a personal decision. You're smart as hell, and frankly if you work as hard as you have been these past few months, you'll climb your way up the ladder at your next company in no time."

"Oh," Cassidy said once more. She had known this was a possibility, she hadn't truly believed it. Her mind was swirling and she couldn't quite formulate the millions of questions she had.

"I know this is not what you had expected, at least not yet."

"No."

"Do you have questions?"

"Oh, um, yeah…" Cassidy scrambled to regain her focus.

"I would expect you have many."

"What happens to my clients? How do I get my final check? Um, do you still provide a reference letter for me to get another job, or is that gone because I'm fired?" she rambled.

"All the clients will be taken care of in-house, you don't need to do anything. We'll mail you your final check -- you'll still be at your current address, right?"

"Yeah," Cassidy nodded, suddenly considering a whole new set of concerns.

"Great. We'll get that out to you first thing next week. And yes, I will still write you a letter of recommendation. You are a reliable employee. College educated and now you have two years under your belt."

"Three," Cassidy corrected.

"Three years of experience in the work force. Your options are limitless!"

"But not here?"

"No, not here."

"Um… okay," Cassidy said. She could feel the bile rising

in her throat. There was a long moment of awkward silence.

"Cassidy," Mr. Jelif said. Cassidy looked up at him. "You really were a good employee. I could always count on you. I just wish you wanted to try harder, not just when the chips are down."

"Yeah." She felt her stomach lurch and her jaw clench.

"And I have to say, you're taking this very gracefully. I know you can be a firecracker, so I wasn't sure how this would go. You've eased my fears for a really hard task -- one I was not looking forward to, no matter the reaction," he admitted.

"What were you expecting?" Cassidy raised an eyebrow.

"I really wasn't sure. Screaming, swearing, maybe throwing a chair through the window."

"It's way too cold to break a window," Cassidy replied flatly. Mr. Jelif failed to cover his chuckle. Cassidy found herself oddly honored. Annoyed. But honored.

"If you have any follow up questions next week, you can call back in. You know my extension – five-nine-three."

"Thanks," Cassidy said in a low voice. "So, I just leave at five and never come back?"

"Well, honestly, you should take a box from the supply cupboard, take any personal items you have out of your desk and head out."

"Now?"

"Yes. I'm sorry, Banker. But it will be easier for you to leave quickly. You don't want to watch your work being divvied up. Trust me," Mr. Jelif said. Cassidy felt like she'd been punched in the gut.

"Okay." Cassidy nodded as she stood up from the chair.

"And while I don't feel like I need to say this to you, after Devon, I am required to say it to everyone: please don't steal any company property. We will take the cost of it out of your final check." Mr. Jelif said. Cassidy paused a moment before realizing she could ask without repercussions.

"What did Devon steal?"

"One of the stone flower pots out front."

"I thought that was taken out by a storm!"

"Nope."

"You charged him for it?"

"And the flowers inside."

"Thank you for telling me." Cassidy gave him a small smile.

"No problem," Mr. Jelif nodded. She gave him a final look before departing his office and going to her desk for the final time.

She was happy she didn't need a box. She was never one for knick-knacks or desk toys. After a quick search through her desk drawers, she pulled out her two packs of gum, a hair claw clip that was painted to look like a golden retriever, and a stress ball with her company's logo on it – a rather apt souvenir, she thought -- and tossed them all into her purse. She put on her coat.

After a few half-assed goodbyes from coworkers, Cassidy left the downtown building and shivered her way to the parking garage across the street.

Chapter 9

The blue Toyota seemed to drive on auto-pilot. That's the only way that Cassidy could explain why she was turning onto her parents' street at this moment. She truly had no recollection of the forty minute drive from the city. She knew she didn't want to go back to the apartment -- she might never leave. So Cassidy drove home. She was planning to be there that evening for dinner, anyway, and she knew both of her parents would be home. Lynne was off because the school she worked at was getting a frozen pipe fixed and the school was closed. The whole ordeal had been quite a scandal among the parents of students. Art had taken a day off in solidarity, or so he said, but Cassidy knew he liked to putz around and fix things that didn't need to be fixed. And if Lynne was home at the same time, he could get her opinion before each new endeavor, rather than her coming home and yelling at him for changing something she loved and making him put it back.

Suddenly, Cassidy was pulling into the long driveway.

It wasn't until Cassidy had turned off the car that she realized she was not fully prepared to tell her parents. Fired. She never imagined she would be fired. It felt like a huge red X across her life. The bile was still lapping her throat. It made her sick. This situation made her feel sick.

After a couple minutes of unhelpful thoughts, Cassidy grabbed her purse and exited the car. She used her key and let herself in the front door.

"Knock, knock!" she called out loudly, not wanting to scare either of her parents -- or herself -- if she walked in on whatever the hell they did without a household of kids. Cassidy had never given it much thought.

"Cassidy?" Art yelled from his study. He sounded surprised.

"Yeah, hi dad."

"Why are you here?" he asked, standing up and making his way into the foyer.

"Felt like coming home a little early today."

"It's four minutes to two. What happened? Ya get fired?" Art joked.

Cassidy froze. She could feel her bottom lip start to quiver. "Oh, no, Cass," Art said, realizing what had happened and opening his arms for a hug. Cassidy didn't hesitate a moment before hugging him tightly.

"What? What's happening? Cassidy? Art, what on earth happened?" Lynne frantically asked as she came from the family room and into the foyer.

"She got the ax," Art said in a painfully loud whisper over his daughter's head before placing a light kiss on her hair.

"Ohhh," Lynne groaned. Cassidy wasn't sure if her mother's reaction was at her situation or her father's gruff announcement. Lynne was never one for kitschy expressions.

"Yeah," Cassidy sighed, pulling back from her father. She wiped her eyes and sniffled. The tears had started. Crap.

"What happened?" Lynne asked gently as she tucked some of her hair behind her ear. Cassidy shrugged.

"The company hasn't been doing great, and well... they've been downsizing really hard. Guess my number was up."

"There you go!" Art said energetically. The Banker women shot him a look. "No, no, see, you weren't fired – it was a downsizing. Still stinks, but it's the company, not you," he explained. Cassidy thought for a moment. He may have been right, but at the moment, it didn't help how she felt.

"It does stink," Cassidy sighed.

"Let me put the kettle on, we'll have some tea and you can sit down and tell me everything," Lynne said, patting her arm. Cassidy gave her a weak smile.

"Okay. But I want to put on something comfortable, at least for a bit. Is there still stuff in my old room?"

"Yeah, go on up. It'll take the water a bit to boil," Lynne said before heading into the kitchen.

"Cassidy," Art said as she was on the second step. She paused and turned to face her father.

"Yeah?"

"I've never seen you all dressed for work. You look like a professional. You're not a kid anymore. Wear this to your interview. You'll knock them dead," Art said. Cassidy grinned at her dad as a few tears slipped out.

"I think this outfit may have the stink of fired on it permanently, but I appreciate your confidence."

"Downsized, Cassidy. Say downsized."

"Either term means jobless."

"Well..."

"Look, I appreciate you trying to cheer me on. I do. But right now, I'm going to go change into my old clothes and just be sad for a bit before I pick my interview outfit."

"Fair enough," Art nodded. Cassidy continued up a few more stairs before turning around once more.

"Dad? Thanks."

"Anytime."

Cassidy spent a couple of hours curled up on the couch in the family room with her mom. She had found some clothes in her old room to change into. She went from professional business woman to slobby chic in a pair of black sweat pants with her high school's logo on the left thigh, a plain white T-shirt that was covered with a bulky red crewneck sweat shirt that said "Edinboro Softball" across the chest in large, white letters, and a pair of ratty pink slippers that Cassidy was pretty sure she got back in middle school. The outfit was symbolic of how she felt at the moment.

Lynne and Cassidy sat together on the large couch in the family room as they drank their tea. They started talking about work, but the conversation turned to updates on cousins, neighbor gossip, asking about Marissa and Jake. Cassidy told her about helping Ellie and Lynne gave her impressions of meeting Mr. and Mrs. Hammond – which differed a bit from Eric's telling, but Cassidy did not tell her that. The easy conversation helped, and the tea was soothing. Cassidy was glad she'd come home early.

A little after five o'clock, Lynne got up to start preparing dinner and Cassidy went upstairs to call Jake and tell him the news from the privacy of her parents' bedroom – the only upstairs telephone.

It only rang twice.

"Hello?"

"Hey, it's me." Cassidy smiled, hearing the familiar voice.

"Hey! Wait… aren't you at your parents' for Matty's birthday?"

"Yeah, I'm here."

"Oh, okay. What's up?" Jake asked.

"Well… I got here early afternoon," Cassidy began slowly.

"Uh huh," Jake gave a low hum. There was a long pause.

"I got fired today," she admitted in a low voice.

"Oh, no," he sounded sad. Cassidy wished she could hug him right now.

"So, I grabbed my stuff and left. I didn't want to go home, I just wanted to go… well, home."

"I'm glad you did," Jake said. Cassidy sniffled.

"It's like I knew it was coming, but it still sucks. I did not expect it today."

"Definitely a surprise to come today."

"It keeps replaying in my head." Cassidy flopped backwards on the bed.

"What did your parents say? Or have you told them yet?"

"I did. They were both off work today."

"So, what did they say?"

"My dad said I should say I was downsized because it's less harsh and puts the fault on the company, not me," Cassidy said. Jake gave a small laugh.

"I love Art."

"Jake," Cassidy whined.

"You don't like that term?"

"I don't know. I don't like this whole situation."

"I get that."

"What am I going to do?" Cassidy asked with a sad sigh. A few tears escaped and she brushed them away with the back of her hand.

"You're going to find a new job."

"I guess."

"Cassidy, I know you're very sad right now, and rightly so, but you'll see. It'll get better!"

"Mmmm."

"Why are you holding back emotions right now?" Jake asked curiously.

"I'm not."

"I know you, Cassandra."

"Not my name."

"I was kidding."

"Go on," she sighed.

"You never hide your feelings. That's what I love about you."

"It does suck!"

"And that you're pretty scared."

"I don't like that."

"I know," Jake said. Cassidy felt a lump in her throat.

"It feels so… embarrassing."

"Yeah, I get that."

"I just don't know what I'm going to do."

"Well, the good and bad news is, it's Friday. You can't do anything until Monday; all businesses will be closed. I'd say just rest this weekend."

"Yeah."

"So, what are you guys doing tonight?" Jake asked.

"Hmm?"

"Matty's birthday," he clarified. Cassidy appreciated a change of subject.

"Oh… probably just dinner and cake. We can't really do anything outside because it's freezing out, and indoor games… well, things get broken."

"I can only imagine," Jake chuckled.

"Well, I need to go change before everyone gets here."

"Change?"

"I was sad; I didn't want to be in the outfit I wore to work."

"You have clothes there?"

"A few left behind. I'm currently in sweats from high school."

"Sounds hot," Jake said. Cassidy snorted.

"Yeah, I'm sure Sports Illustrated will call me for their swimsuit edition any second now."

"Better hang up and not hog the line then."

"Thank you," Cassidy said in a heartfelt voice after a long pause.

"For thinking you're hot?"

"No. Well, that's nice, too, but, for being what I needed right now."

"Of course. Anytime, always."

"I love you."

"I love you, too," Jake said. "Call me when you get home tonight. Or are you staying in Meadville?"

"The only thing that would make me feel sadder than being fired--"

"Downsized," Jake interrupted. Cassidy rolled her eyes.

"The only thing that will make me feel worse than being fired," she enunciated. "is staying in my old bedroom with my parents fussing over me like I'm two."

"That's not the worst thing."

"Ugh. I know," Cassidy groaned. "I'm just feeling… shitty."

"That's fair," Jake said. "Do me a favor though, huh? Don't drive home if you aren't in the right headspace. I think we're getting some snow."

"We always have snow. And I will be in the right headspace if you agree to come over tonight," Cassidy grinned.

"Call me when you get home."

"Okay."

"Love you."

"Love you, too," Cassidy said as she hung up the phone.

At six o'clock, Cassidy was back downstairs in the kitchen, leaning on the island as she watched her mother chop vegetables for the salad. Lynne had absolutely forbidden Cassidy from helping, which was a mixture of nice and really boring.

After Cassidy talked to Jake, she changed out of the sweatpants and back into her skirt and stockings, but kept her sweatshirt on. It was chilly.

"When are they getting here?" Cassidy asked, twirling a fork on the countertop.

"You sound like your father."

"Thank you," Cassidy grinned, taking it like a huge compliment. Lynne groaned, making her daughter laugh.

"They show up whenever they show up… you all do," Lynne said pointedly.

"Hey! I'm sad."

"I know, I know," Lynne stopped chopping for a moment to give Cassidy a kiss on her temple. "And honestly, I'm so glad that you came here to us and not to some dingy bar, or dark alley, or strip club."

"What?" Cassidy looked confused.

"I don't know what you kids do," Lynne smirked.

"Well, my strip club in the dark alley got busted for crack last week," Cassidy replied smartly.

"Okay, okay, that was dumb of me."

"Only a little."

"Fine, but I'm glad you aren't blowing money in a bar when you won't have an income for a bit."

"Why do you think I'm here? The drinks are free," Cassidy winked, holding up a bottle of beer. Lynne was about to say something when they were interrupted by the sound of the door opening.

"Hi!" Matty called out. Lynne dropped the knife and hurried to the foyer. Cassidy remained in the kitchen and listened.

"Birthday boy!"

"Thanks, mom."

"Is that Cassidy's car here? She's never here first," Matty asked. Cassidy rolled her eyes.

"It is," Lynne said normally before dropping her voice to a loud whisper that wasn't as inconspicuous as she clearly hoped. "Matty, I need you to be really nice to your sister today; she's having a hard time. I don't want to make a big deal about it, but she lost her job this afternoon."

"I can hear you!" Cassidy yelled from the kitchen. She heard Matty chuckle as they both came into the room.

"Sweetie, I'm sorry. I'm just concerned," Lynne said in a

gentle voice as she tucked a lock of hair behind Cassidy's right ear.

"So, you got canned?" Matty asked, his head tilted slightly. Cassidy sighed.

"Yep."

"Just for my birthday?" he asked sarcastically, dramatically bringing his hand to his heart. Cassidy laughed despite herself.

"Sorry I didn't wrap it."

"I can put a bow on your head."

"Perfect," Cassidy smirked. Matty suddenly grabbed her shoulders and pulled her in for a too-tight hug. Cassidy grunted as she fell into him.

"Sweet, thoughtful, little sister," he cooed.

"Yeah, yeah," Cassidy sighed, firmly patting his back. He was just starting to let her go when the front door slammed and Ben bounded into the room.

"Oh, God," he gasped, shocked to see his siblings hugging. It was a rare sight, at least with Matty. "Who died?"

"No one," Cassidy pushed herself back.

"Just Cassidy's career and prospects," Matty said.

"Shut up."

"Matthew!" Lynne scolded. Cassidy punched him hard in the arm.

"Whoa," Ben breathed, surprised at the exchange.

"When's dinner?" Cassidy asked her mother, desperate for a distraction.

"Thirty minutes, at least. And not everyone is here yet."

"Eric's here," Ben said.

"Where?" Matty asked.

"Outside. We got here at the same time, but Dad asked him to help get the driveway salt out of the back of his car," Ben said.

"What? Why would he ask him to do that now?" Lynne grumbled. She quickly wiped her hands on her apron before stomping over to the door to the garage on the other side of the kitchen.

"Uh, oh," Cassidy, Matt, and Ben all hummed in unison.

"Art! What are you guys doing? Get inside, it's freezing out!" Lynne barked.

"Almost done!" Art called back.

"Hey, mom!" Eric greeted.

"Hi, sweetie."

"We'll be in soon, just giving him a head's up about… you know, and to be extra nice to her," Art said in a voice that managed to echo through the air. Cassidy rolled her eyes.

"Subtle."

"Amazing," Matty gave a low chuckle.

"Arthur! She's right here!" Lynne hissed.

"Oh," Art said in surprise.

"Just get inside," Lynne ordered. The sound of the large, double garage door whirring as it closed could be heard, and a few moments later Art and Eric entered the kitchen.

"Sorry, Cassidy," Art said sheepishly.

"Eh," Cassidy shrugged.

"Happy birthday, Matt!" Eric said cheerily before giving his sister a weak smile. Cassidy bit her tongue. She knew he meant well, but she hated feeling pitied.

"Thanks!" Matty beamed.

"Yeah, Happy birthday!" Ben patted his arm. "But what happened to Cassidy?"

"She was downsized today," Art explained.

"What?" Ben asked.

79

"Ben, I got fired," Cassidy said with a loud exhale.

"Downsized, it was their fault," Art interjected.

"Dad, that doesn't actually help," Cassidy countered.

"That sucks," Ben said, scrunching his face slightly.

"See, he gets it," she said, gesturing to her youngest brother. "And Matty, stop looking so happy! It's not funny anymore." She skulked off to the small powder room off the hallway.

She heard her name being called as she shut the bathroom door. She ignored everyone. Cassidy took a seat on the closed toilet seat lid and leaned forward. Placing her head in her hands and balancing her elbows on her knees.

"Lord, help me," she whispered. She could feel her body clench in frustration, humiliation, anger, and the twenty-six other emotions she was experiencing right now. After a couple of minutes feeling sorry for herself, she stood up and splashed water on her face. She looked at her reflection as she patted her face dry with the hand towel. She didn't look like herself.

"Get your shit together, Banker," Cassidy said to her reflection before flushing the unused toilet and exiting the small powder room.

Lynne was back working away in the kitchen and Art and the boys had moved to the family room where they were all lounging and arguing as Ben flipped through the channels with the remote. Cassidy decided to return to the kitchen.

"Hey mom."

"I'm sorry, sweetie," Lynne said as she opened the oven to peek inside.

"It's okay," Cassidy shrugged.

"Really? I would expect you to be a lot more upset."

"What happened to the calm down, Cassidy speech you normally give?"

"You're usually much louder, and the infraction against you much smaller," Lynne replied calmly. Cassidy shot her a look.

"Maybe I'm in shock."

"Maybe."

"Can I just ask one favor, please?"

"What's that?"

"Can you stop looking at me like I have cancer?"

"What?" Lynne asked, looking shocked.

"The pity party... I can't stand the sad puppy looks. They make me feel worse than I already do. Let me just enjoy dinner and give Matty all the attention that he loves," Cassidy said. Lynne smiled at her.

"Okay."

"Oh, and the whispering doesn't work. If you want to talk about me, wait until I'm not in the house. You're not good at being secretive."

"Alright," Lynne agreed.

"Thank you."

"You're welcome."

"So, what is for dinner tonight?" Cassidy asked.

"Matty's favorite, of course – chicken parmigiana!"

"Mmm, oh! Matty!" Cassidy gasped.

"What?"

"I never brought his gift in from the car when I got here," Cassidy said as she scurried around the kitchen island. She ran to the front door and swung it open only to be hit by a gust of cold air.

"Ugh!" Cassidy groaned before shutting the door. She opened the coat closet and grabbed the first thing she could find, which happened to be her mom's navy blue peacoat. Her shoes were still upstairs in her old room, so she slipped into her father's brown snow boots before opening the door once more and hopping out onto the porch. The shoes were big and she felt a bit like a toddler, but at least she was warm.

Cassidy hobbled ungracefully out to her car, grabbed the orange gift bag out of her backseat – three brand new cassettes -- and slammed the car door closed just as a white Honda pulled into the end of the driveway. Alex, late as usual. Cassidy held her spot and waited for him.

"Wow, love the new look there, Oscar Madison!" Alex chuckled as he got out of his car.

"You're not exactly Felix," Cassidy smirked.

"Why are you in dad's shoes?"

"Because I forgot Matty's present in my car and had to run out and get it, and it's really cold out."

"Where are your shoes?"

"My room."

"Your old room here? Why the hell were you in there?" Alex asked as they slowly walked onto the porch together. Cassidy sighed. She had to tell him. Better from her than Matty.

"Well… um… I got fired today," Cassidy said. She looked up at him, grimacing slightly. Alex looked horrified.

"Cassie, I'm so sorry."

"I mean, it sucks."

"Yeah," he said, opening the front door for them. The foyer felt delightfully warm.

"Cassidy?" Lynne asked from the kitchen. They set their presents for Matty on the steps while they removed their coats and Cassidy slipped out of her father's boots.

"Alex is here, too," Cassidy called.

"Oh, good, perfect timing!"

"Hi, mom," Alex said, but Lynne was already running the other way to get the rest of the guys out of the family room. "Has she been frantic?" he asked in a low voice. Cassidy nodded.

"Yes. Everyone has been very sad... Well, except for Matty. He's downright thrilled," Cassidy rolled her eyes. Alex scoffed before pulling her into a gentle hug.

"He's sad for you, he's just an asshole."

"It's fine," Cassidy said as she relaxed against him.

"Remember, you can stay with me and Laura before you have to move back with mom and dad."

"I appreciate that," Cassidy said truthfully. She had been trying not to think of what her housing situation might be next month. Alex rested his head on hers.

"Hey!" Matty yelled as he walked into the foyer.

"Happy birthday!" Alex smiled at him as he and Cassidy slowly pulled apart.

"Why is she nice to you? I tried to hug her today and she punched me," Matty acted offended.

"Because you crushed my organs," Cassidy pointed out as she pushed between her brothers and went into the kitchen to help her mom get everything on the table.

Dinner was delicious and a lot of fun. Jokes were flying back and forth, and, at one point, Ben's spoon. They all enjoyed hearty helpings of ice cream cake and giving Matty his birthday gifts, before moving into the family room for a game Outburst. They made it through a miraculous four rounds before their first argument, and the game didn't have to be forcefully ended until round seven. While the teams were neck and neck, the category "Things Left in Space" turned into a very surprising debate, lots of insults, and a few far-fetched conspiracy theories. However, the game ending clincher was Ben angrily throwing the game card reader into the lit fireplace and Eric punching him for doing so.

Art fished the card reader out of the fire with the tongs, but there was nothing to salvage, so he tossed it back in, despite Lynne's annoyance.

Once everything was put away, everyone started to gather their things. Cassidy ran upstairs to her childhood bedroom to retrieve her shoes, as well as her work blouse and purse. She took a moment to sit on her bed and look around her bedroom. She let out a deep sigh as she took in the familiar surroundings, listening to the chatter and chaos from downstairs.

Cassidy chewed on her lip as her mind swirled. She could find herself living back home by early next year. She tried hard to remind herself that her situation could be worse. She could be facing actual homelessness. While she was grateful for her family, it was hard to swallow the fact that sleeping in her childhood bedroom as she struggled to find a job was a very real possibility for her future. Ben was graduating from college next spring. Would he move back for a bit, too? Would she be down the hall from her baby brother once more? Who would get a job first?

Her mind started to spin faster and faster with questions she didn't want answers to. The lump in her throat formed once more.

"Ugh, fuck off," Cassidy said in a low voice, speaking to the thoughts in her head, the lump in her throat -- hell, to the whole situation.

"I didn't even say anything!"

Cassidy jolted and turned to see Matty leaning in her open doorway.

"Ah! How long have you been there?"

"Not long enough to warrant a fuck off," he said flatly. Cassidy sighed.

"What do you want?"

"I'm heading out."

"Okay." There was a long pause. "And happy birthday."

"Thanks."

"Hmm?"

"I'm sorry you lost your job," Matty said in a serious tone. Cassidy looked up at him for a moment. He wasn't sincere very often, but when he was it always hit her hard. Perhaps that was the point?

"Thanks. I appreciate that." She gave him a small smile.

"Okay, well, you'll get back on your feet. You always do."

"I hope so."

"Don't start being humble and meek now. You walk into an interview acting like a candy-ass, you'll never get a job. Not to mention, you can't really pull that look off," Matty said.

"What? Unemployed and homeless?"

"No, insecure."

"Oh. Is that a compliment?" Cassidy asked. Matty shrugged.

"More of a fact. You've always been cocky – mostly because you can back it up with skill, but self-doubt doesn't suit you. Knock it off."

"Matty, I'm sad!"

"I know."

"So, I can't be sad?"

"You can, but don't stay there."

"But—"

"Cassidy, it's my birthday and you're making me be way too nice to you," Matty said playfully. Cassidy smiled at him.

"Okay, you've served your time," she laughed.

"Okay." He smiled at her. "Now, get your shit and come downstairs."

"Why?" Cassidy asked.

"Because Alex wants to take you home, and his car is blocking most of us in."

"I have my car."

"I know, but he thinks you'll cry and not pay attention, hit some black ice and end up in a snowbank or something dramatic like that," Matty said, waving his arms emphatically.

"It's mostly highway, roads will be treated."

"Look, no one here would like to see you on the news for flipping your car and getting wedged somewhere dumb more than me. But if that happens, I will have to listen to Alex tell me that he was right for the rest of my life. And well, I cant -- no, I won't -- let that happen. So, please, get in his car and act grateful," Matty instructed. Cassidy fought hard to hold back a laugh.

"I'm coming, but I can still drive," Cassidy said as she grabbed her things and stood up.

"Shut up or I'll put you in his trunk," Matty said as he followed her down the hallway and down the stairs.

"Oh please! You couldn't fight me to get me in."

"I wouldn't fight you, I'd knock you unconscious."

"You'd still have to lift me into the trunk. That's dead weight. Ain't happening with your skinny arms."

"Bet you five bucks I could. There's a skillet in the kitchen I could hit you with," Matty said as the stepped off the bottom step into the foyer.

"No one is hitting anyone," Lynne said, overhearing the last bit of the conversation.

"And definitely not for a five dollar bet," Cassidy said pointedly.

"Name your price; bet the guys will pitch in," Matty said, pointing at their siblings.

"What are we pitching in for?" Eric asked.

"I'm not paying for any idea you have," Ben said. His nose had finally stopped bleeding, but it was still pretty swollen. Lynne had held an ice pack to it for the last fifteen minutes, and now the skin was red and irritated -- from the hit and the cold. He was looking slightly pathetic, if Cassidy was honest.

"He wants to put me in Alex's trunk," Cassidy remarked.

"I'll go in for ten," Eric said.

"Eric," Cassidy whined, reaching over to slap his chest. He already had his coat on, so it didn't faze him at all.

"I'll put her in there for free," Ben smiled.

"I can make your eye match your nose," Cassidy warned.

"Why is she going in my trunk?" Alex asked as he retrieved his coat from the closet behind them.

"None of you are going in anyone's truck," Lynne said loudly. Clearly she was ready for some peace and quiet in her house once more. Everyone got the hint that it was time to leave. Hugs and goodbyes filled the foyer as the seven of them shuffled around prior to departing. Cassidy was very aware her goodbye hugs were a little longer than usual. Her parents, even Ben and Matty. She couldn't lie, it was nice.

"Sorry, Cas," Eric said seriously.

"Thanks," Cassidy gave her twin a small smile.

"Call me sometime, we'll have a drink," Eric said.

"I'd like that," Cassidy replied honestly before giving him a hug and he headed out the door behind Matty and Ben. Cassidy stepped out on the porch and saw Alex having a cigarette, leaning on the banister.

"Come on, you're holding everyone up," Alex said, exhaling a large puff of smoke.

"I'm parked in," Cassidy said, pointing to her Toyota at the front of the line, closest to the garage door. Alex shook his head.

"Let me drive you home."

"Alex…"

"Please?"

"Why?"

"Because in ten minutes you're going to be in tears," Alex said. Cassidy bit her tongue. She was annoyed that he was right. And while she had driven while crying before, it was dark, cold, well below freezing, and the air smelled like snow. Cassidy knew that having an emotional breakdown while driving would not be in her best interest right now. And if she did crash – who would find her? How would she get ahold of anyone? It was stark driving between Meadville and Erie. Her best options were to ride with Alex or to sleep in her old room as her parents bickered and hovered outside her door. Cassidy took option A.

"Okay… But you'd better have tissues in your car," Cassidy told Alex. He smiled smugly before taking his final drag and pitching the cigarette butt into the dirt.

"There's a box in the backseat. Laura had a cold last week and I drove her to the doctor's."

"Okay." She followed Alex to his car.

Both Ben and Matty had parked behind Cassidy and were

able to drive away. Eric was parked next to Cassidy -- the only one blocked in by Alex's stalling.

"Thank God," Eric sighed seeing them walk to the car. His arms were resting on the hood of the car as he stood there, waiting to be freed.

"Sorry," Alex said, patting Eric's shoulder as he walked to his car. Cassidy gave Eric a shrug as they shared a look before both getting into their cars and out of the cold.

Chapter 10

"It's colder in here than outside," Cassidy shivered, rubbing her arms in her coat.

"Give it a minute, it'll warm up," Alex said as they turned out of their parents' neighborhood. "I'm assuming you won't let me open the window to smoke once we get out on 79?"

"Absolutely not! You can wait forty-five minutes."

Alex groaned; Cassidy ignored him. If it was any other season, she wouldn't care, but if it was cold enough to snow, she would make him go without.

"Alex, you'll make it."

"What about you?"

"I'll be fine without a cigarette. I've smoked maybe four or five times in my life. I don't even have a habit to kick," Cassidy chuckled.

"I meant since losing your job," Alex clarified.

"I mean, it sucks."

"Yeah."

"What do you want me to say?"

"You can say whatever you want!"

"I feel like you want me to fall apart."

"I don't want you to, but it would make sense."

"Matty said you were going to drive me."

"And you took the offer," Alex said.

"Like I had a choice without throwing a fit!"

"You like throwing fits," he shrugged. Cassidy shot him a glare.

"I feel like you're baiting me right now. Pushing so I get mad."

"Cassidy, I asked how you were going to manage," Alex sighed as he put on his turn signal for the on ramp of the highway.

"Why did Matty say you were going to drive me home?" Cassidy asked.

"Because I said I was going to." The car accelerated as he merged in front of a station wagon.

"So, everyone was talking about me when I left the room?"

"About today's occurrence, yes."

"Oh."

"Cassidy, despite everything, we all do love you and we're sad that you lost your job. It's a big deal."

"No! No, its not," Cassidy said, looking out the passenger side window at the dark fields surrounding the highway. That annoying feeling was back: her stomach turning and her throat hurting. She felt herself excessively blinking. She swallowed hard.

"How is it not?"

"Because it's a job. There are people with cancer and, and…" her mind was drawing a blank. "And other real problems."

"Why are you downplaying it?"

"I'm not!" Cassidy shot back. She felt like she was being backed into a corner.

"Okay," Alex hummed in a sing-song voice.

"The heat is finally working in here. Would you be less of a dick if I told you to smoke the rest of the drive?" Cassidy growled.

"I'm going to let you have that one… but only that one," Alex warned. Cassidy swallowed hard.

"Stop. Pushing. Please." she said in a voice just above a whisper.

"I just want a simple answer."

"No, you want a really hard answer because I have no idea what I'm going to do," Cassidy choked out. A few tears escaped. She hated this feeling. Falling apart. Especially when she was falling apart because the world she knew was crumbling. Her heart hurt.

"There we go," Alex said in a kind voice, looking over at her. Cassidy knew that look. It was how he looked at her when they were kids and she wasn't allowed to do something because she was a girl, or not big enough. It was the pity face. And it went right through her. It was the face he made when he knew exactly how lousy and sad she felt. The older she got, the more she hated it. She hated looking sad or weak. The rare times she ever felt that way, she could hide it from most people. But Alex saw her. Raw and broken. She couldn't hide right now, and couldn't run, unless she was prepared for injury from tucking and rolling followed by frost bite, which she was not. Cassidy was stuck. In the car. In her emotions. In her brokenness. It sucked.

"You're enjoying this, aren't you?" Cassidy said as she started to cry.

"Not at all," Alex said. Cassidy sniffled loudly. "I hate that this happened to you."

"But...?"

"But, you can't hold it all in; it'll kill you," he said. Cassidy cried quietly, shaky breaths and sniffles, really. She felt pathetic. She continued to whimper for about a minute. An old Bee Gees song came on the radio, and Alex actively tried not to hum along. Cassidy finally took a big breath.

"But if I let myself fall apart ... it is real," she sniffled.

"Cassie, it is real. Your job is gone," Alex said in a low voice. And that was it. Her heart sank. The flood gates opened and she cried. Hard. "There it is," Alex hummed sadly.

Her tears streamed as she sobbed. Alex reached back and passed her the box of tissues before turning up the radio and continuing to drive. Honestly, she appreciated it. Cassidy felt her body tremble as she cried. She hated feeling this out of control. A few heavy sobs made her think she might even throw up, but was able to settle herself.

Four songs, two radio sales jingles, and an interlude of DJ banter later, Cassidy's sobbing ceased. She was back to low sniffles as she dried her face, which was now feeling very chapped, and blew her nose, causing her to give a few, slightly pathetic coughs.

"Whoa," Cassidy sighed.

"Hmm?" Alex hummed, glancing over at her before returning his eyes to the road.

"It's snowing," she replied flatly as she looked out the window. Alex gave a snort.

"Yep."

Cassidy took a few shaky breaths and blew her nose again before repositioning so she was sitting cross-legged on the passenger seat with her feet tucked underneath her. She smoothed her skirt over her knees.

"How much longer?" she asked as she ran her fingers through her hair.

"Twenty minutes. Maybe a bit more."

"Okay."

"How do you feel?"

"Um… snotty," Cassidy answered honestly and grabbed another tissue.

"I think that's step one," Alex teased.

"Good for me," Cassidy replied sarcastically.

"You should feel lighter."

"Lighter?" Cassidy tilted her head as she looked at him. "Oh, because I'm losing so much snot?" Alex snorted.

"No. I'm not Matty."

"That is a solid Matty joke. I'll have to call and tell him it tomorrow."

"He would appreciate that," Alex smiled. A peaceful silence fell between the two for a long minute.

"You know, yeah," Cassidy began.

"What?" Alex asked. "Cassie, you can't just start talking mid-sentence, I don't live in your head."

"I know!" And thank goodness you don't Cassidy thought to herself.

"So?"

"So, I actually feel like a weight has lifted."

"Good," Alex said.

"I mean, I still feel sad… and kind of freaked out… and well--"

"Well?"

"Well, if I think about it, I'll get all worked up again," Cassidy admitted.

"I mean, it did just happen today."

"True," Cassidy shrugged. "Distract me."

"What?"

"You got your way, I cried."

"I wasn't cheering it on," Alex rolled his eyes.

"Okay, but you were right, I needed that," she admitted. "But now I need something else to think about."

"Um…"

"Tell me something that you and Laura are doing this weekend."

"We're going to go see her parents on Sunday."

"Are her parents actually hippies?"

"Cassie…"

"Sorry, but is it true they actually went to Woodstock?"

"Yeah," Alex smiled.

"Wow! They must have the coolest stories."

"Some are pretty crazy."

"Tell me one. Please? I'm sad," Cassidy said. Alex laughed before diving into Laura's dad, Gerald's, favorite story of them accidentally joining a playful mud sliding competition between a group of friends. They were trying to find their tent and when scrambling up a small hill, Gerald lost his footing and stumbled, knocking his wife, Shirley, down in the process. Shirley slid headfirst down the other side next to a man from Ohio, who was quite surprised to see her there. The group from Ohio liked her slide and invited Gerald and Shirley to join their game! Gerald and Shirley spent the next hour rolling down the hill with their new friends. Gerald managed to lose one of his shoes in the process. When making a pitstop in the river to rinse off before restarting their journey to find their tent, Gerald spotted a lone shoe on the bank and took it. He spent the rest of the festival in mismatched shoes.

The story made both Cassidy and Alex laugh, and prompted tales of childhood car trip disasters, which were plentiful. The final twenty minutes of the ride were filled with laughter and contentment, which was good, as Alex had to lower his speed considerably due to the snow. But they made it back to Cassidy's apartment in one piece.

Despite Cassidy's assurance that she would make it inside without incident, Alex walked her to her door. While Cassidy appreciated her eldest brother more than she usually showed, sometimes his overprotective nature took odd turns. What did he think she was going to do? Hurl herself down one flight of stairs?

With Alex in tow, Cassidy made her way to the second floor and let herself into her apartment.

"Hi," she called, kicking off her shoes and hanging up her thick winter coat on the hook by the door.

"Hey," Marissa said looking sad, her hand over her heart.

"What's happening?" Cassidy asked with a raised eyebrow.

"Jake told me about work."

"What?"

"Hey," Jake emerged from the far side of the living room with a small smile. Cassidy was so happy to see him.

"I thought you were coming over later," Cassidy said as she hurried over to him and hugged him, wrapping her arms around his middle. She took a deep breath, her face buried in his shoulder. Her whole body relaxed as he hugged her back.

"Well, I thought it would be nice to see you when you got home," Jake said, slowly pulling out of the hug. "Hey, Alex."

"Hey." Alex gave a nod. He didn't look thrilled to see Cassidy clinging to him, but still much friendlier than their first meeting.

"Yeah, hi, Alex, it's been forever," Marissa said, leaning over to give Alex a quick side hug which he happily returned.

"Yeah, been a while."

"Did you drive her back?" Jake asked Alex, stepping away from Cassidy. Cassidy knew he was trying not to push his luck.

"Yeah. Couldn't have her ending up in a snowbank," Alex shrugged.

"Appreciate that." Jake gave a low chuckle.

"You guys have no faith in me," Cassidy said.

"I'm sorry, but how many used tissues are in your purse right now? Thirty?" Alex asked.

"Ugh, probably. I need to clean that out," Cassidy grimaced as the other three laughed.

"Alex, are you staying for a drink?" Marissa asked.

"I appreciate the offer, but the snow is picking up. I want to get home," Alex said.

"Okay. Drive safe and thank you for the ride," Cassidy said sincerely.

"I'll call you tomorrow," Alex told her.

"Sounds good. Tell Laura I said hi."

"Will do."

"Stay for drink when it's not snowing," Marissa told him. Alex grinned.

"Definitely."

Cassidy smiled at her brother and gave a small wave. However, he wasn't looking at her, but over her shoulder. He was looking at Jake. Alex jerked his head towards the door and Cassidy looked back to see Jake nod.

"I'll be right back," Jake said, giving her a quick peck before following Alex out the door of the apartment.

"What the hell?" Cassidy asked, looking at Marissa as she walked past her into their galley kitchen.

"Oh, who knows," Marissa said with a shrug as she stood on her tip toes and pulled a bottle of wine off the top of the fridge. "Who cares, it's time for wine!"

"I care," Cassidy sighed as she came over and leaned against the counter to watch Marissa open the bottle.

"Tell me what happened."

"How much did Jake tell you?"

"Not much."

"He just showed up?"

"He called about an hour ago. I told him you weren't here yet and he asked if he could come over and wait for you."

"Oh," Cassidy said as Marissa gave a grunt, finally dislodging the cork form the bottle.

"He said you invited him over and he was worried because you lost your job today," Marissa said as she placed three wine glasses on the counter and started to pour.

"Thanks for letting him come over."

"Yeah, Jake and I are cool."

"And nice of you to pour him a glass," Cassidy smiled, taking the stem of the glass that Marissa pushed toward her.

"Hey, I'm not a complete airhead… Not to mention, he's the one that brought this bottle," Marissa winked. Cassidy laughed.

"Ahh, so, sharing."

"I'm very nice," Marissa grinned. The girls laughed as they clinked their glasses together and took a sip.

"Ugh, where are they?" Cassidy asked, leaning back slightly to try and see the door.

"Ignore them," Marissa waved, walking to the living room and taking a seat on the oversized chair. Cassidy flopped down on the couch, accidentally sloshing her wine. A few drops spilled onto her sweatshirt from home.

"Shit."

"Yeah, I have to ask about the outfit," Marissa said, taking another sip.

"Well, I was dressed nice for work. I was planning to stop here before going to my parents' place, but, well, I got fired at lunch and just high-tailed it home. Found this in my old room," Cassidy sighed.

"Fair," Marissa nodded. "Don't you have, like, a box of your stuff from your desk? I see that in TV when people are fired."

"I didn't have many personal things there. Some are in my purse, some are in my car, but not enough for a box. Thank God."

"Where's your car?"

"At my parents'. I'll see if Jake can drive me back tomorrow to grab it."

"If he can't go, I'll drive you back. I'm not meeting Brandon until dinner," Marissa said.

"Thanks," Cassidy smiled.

"Now, how did it go down?" Marissa asked. Before Cassidy could answer, there was a loud knock at the door.

"Must be Jake," Cassidy said, heaving herself off the couch

and letting him in.

"Sorry, locked myself out," Jake grinned when Cassidy opened the door. He was annoyingly cute.

"It's okay. I heard you brought wine," Cassidy said as she turned to walk back to the living room.

"And I see you've opened it," Jake teased, shutting the door behind him and following her to the couch.

"We poured you a glass," Marissa said, pointing to the counter.

"Thank you." He quickly grabbed the glass and settled in the middle of the couch. Cassidy curled up against him.

"What did Alex want?" Cassidy asked, taking another drink.

"Not much," Jake shrugged.

"Liar! Boooo!" Marissa called loudly making Jake jump slightly before looking down at Cassidy, who was grinning.

"Jeez!"

"This is why she's my friend," Cassidy replied smugly.

"Yeah," Jake hummed as he looked warily at Marissa.

"So?" Cassidy asked.

"He just asked me to keep an eye on you. He's really worried," Jake said. Cassidy knew she should be touched, but she gritted her teeth.

"I love him, but he treats me like I'm suicidal. I'm not. I swear."

"I'm glad to hear it," Jake said.

"What happened?" Marissa asked. Cassidy sighed and retold the whole story. It felt just as terrible in the retelling. However, the addition of wine was nice. Jake and Marissa listened to her saga with full attention, and sympathetic faces, which made Cassidy feel both better and worse. From her firing to her afternoon with her parents, she went over every detail. Marissa refilled their wine glasses, and Jake rubbed her back. Cassidy felt good that she only teared up twice. While Marissa had been there for multiple meltdowns and break-up cries over the years, this was her first time crying in front of Jake. He held up well.

"Want to come over next week? I can help you with your resume," Jake offered after a long pause.

"Yeah... Yeah, I guess I need to start job searching. Is the paper still here or did you throw that out?" Cassidy asked with a sigh.

"Don't look now," Marissa said firmly.

"Yeah, no. Take the weekend," Jake agreed.

"I feel like I should jump-start this," Cassidy said.

"Next week," Jake said, kissing her cheek. Marissa jumped in and changed the subject to the recent news reports that England and France were trying to dig some tunnel under the water to connect the countries. Marissa and Cassidy both found it preposterous; however, Jake was very interested how they would manage it.

Two hours later, Cassidy was showered, in pajamas, and curled up in bed in her dark bedroom next to Jake.

"Thanks for coming over tonight," Cassidy whispered.

"It's going to be okay," Jake said, rubbing his thumb gently on her cheek.

"Is it? When?"

"Well, not right now."

"Yeah."

"Cassidy, this is a set-back, not permanent."

"I just don't want to have to move back home."

"That's not the worst thing."

"It feels like a massive step back."

"It would be a small step back, and it hasn't even happened yet."

"But…"

"Babe, today sucked, but it doesn't mean your life will," Jake said. Cassidy sighed and leaned forward, resting her forehead on his shoulder. Jake held her close and kissed her cheek.

"So," Cassidy said after a long moment, bringing her head back to her pillow, "are you still going to love an unemployed mooch?"

"I think I can make that work," Jake winked. Cassidy placed a soft kiss on his lips.

"And I can find work," she said determinedly.

"Yes. Yes, you can," Jake agreed, giving her one more kiss before they both settled into comfortable positions and fell into a deep and restful sleep.

Chapter 11

Cassidy was heading into her second week of unemployment, and she was not thriving. Jake helped her update her resume and they worked on a cover letter while Marissa helped her pick out some professional outfits. Scouring the newspaper and dropping off her resume and cover letter at multiple accounting firms and companies with finance departments had proven fruitless. The ones that were hiring gave her an unconvincing 'We'll be in touch,' and the others seemed to have zero interest in doing any hiring before the upcoming holidays. Cassidy couldn't blame them. The middle of December was not ideal for job searching.

Cassidy had returned to her parents' house the night before for dinner. She didn't have anything else to do, and she was getting anxious about eating too much food at the apartment. How was she going to afford groceries? She couldn't make Marissa pay for her share.

After a delicious meal and another emotional breakdown

from Cassidy, Art had sat her down in his office and offered her a deal. He would loan her money until she got back on her feet with a new job, and she could pay him back as she was able to. His only stipulation was that she was not to use money to go out and party or blow on frivolous shopping trips. The loan was for necessities only. Cassidy asked about Christmas. She had planned to do all of her shopping the weekend she was fired. Obviously, that hadn't worked out.

Art advised her to offer non-tangible gifts – her time and help. Everyone knew her current situation and no one would expect expensive gifts. He told her that her grandfathers and great-grandfathers, most of whom were factory workers, gave gifts of service many years when they didn't have money, and they were always greatly appreciated. Cassidy smiled at the thought. She had never met any of her great grandparents, but still had her paternal grandfather: a strong, determined, and an extraordinarily hard-working man. He had been so proud of her father – the first of the family to go to college.

She was incredibly grateful for her family, not only for her upbringing, but for their generosity. She was lucky. Not only was she not homeless, but she didn't even have to move back home. Granted, she could already hear Matty quip that they didn't want her back home. And while he could be right, Cassidy cried as she hugged her father with deep gratitude. She promised to search even harder for a job and pay him back, with interest, the second she could. Art kissed her head and said he knew she would.

Cassidy had had yet another tearful drive home from her parents, but that night, they were tears of joy and immense gratefulness.

The next day, December 15th, was the first day of Hanukkah.

Cassidy was seated in the living room with Marissa, Brandon, and Jake. Cassidy had been celebrating Hanukkah with Marissa since their first year as roommates back in 1981 -- sophomore year at Edinboro. While Cassidy was not Jewish, she liked supporting Marissa in her faith. Marissa, in turn, had attended multiple Christmas Eve services with her over the years at the Lutheran Church. Cassidy had come to truly enjoy celebrating Hanukkah, even memorizing a few of the Hebrew phrases. Not to mention, it was significantly more fun than observing Yom Kippur. That was rough. She'd made it through two years of that with Marissa before politely asking to skip future years. Marissa had taken it well.

This wasn't the first year others had joined them for holiday. Depending on when the holiday fell each year, Marissa wasn't always able to go home. Often it was during finals week at school, so she couldn't travel. This year her parents were in Ohio with her older sister, Julie, her husband, and their baby daughter to celebrate with them, as it was her niece's first Hanukkah.

Marissa invited Brandon, who was slightly confused about what the holiday entailed, but he was won over when Marissa explained what latkes were. And when Cassidy told Jake they were celebrating, he immediately asked for an invitation, citing not only the potato latkes and jelly doughnuts, but true interest in the holiday.

Despite Cassidy being home all day with nothing to do but help prep, Marissa took the day off work to cook. Cassidy appreciated the company, and the opportunity to actually do something! Although Marissa took charge and gave Cassidy more of the minor tasks, Cassidy was thrilled for an activity that wasn't job searching or wallowing.

"So, how does this go?" Jake asked Marissa now that all four were in the living room and the delicious aromas of holiday food filled the air.

"I light the menorah and then recite the Shehecheyanu. I won't make you do any chants, though."

"Darn," Brandon interjected sarcastically, causing Marissa to smack his knee.

"And then we eat, exchange gifts, and play games," Marissa finished with a smile.

"It's fun!" Cassidy grinned.

"That all sounds great, but I have to ask… what are you reciting?" Jake asked.

"Shehecheyanu."

"Sheh-what?" Jake asked delicately.

"She-hek-ee-yah-new," Marissa pronounced slowly. Both the boys spoke along slowly after her. Cassidy had to laugh. She'd done the same thing her first year (or three) of celebrating.

"Okay, okay," Cassidy cut in. "Do the honors!" She passed Marissa a box of matches. Marissa struck a match and lit the shamash before lighting the first candle.

"Do we clap?" Brandon asked in a whisper.

"No, but thank you for the enthusiasm," Marissa said as she kissed him on the cheek and then blew out the match. She recited the Shehecheyanu blessing and a prayer before they dug into the loads of food that filled their kitchen and Marissa taught them how to play traditional games. The gift exchange was done white-elephant style, which Marissa firmly insisted was not how it was supposed to be done, but since she was celebrating with two Lutherans and a lapsed Catholic, she let it slide.

The night was fun and filled with laughter, delicious food, and people Cassidy loved. It was exactly what she needed.

The next seven nights of Hanukkah were just as fun, even though Jake couldn't make a few of them. Cassidy appreciated the distraction of the holiday. She applied for more jobs in the area, all with similar results. No one wanted to think seriously about hiring right before the holidays.

Jake agreed to her suggestion of non-monetary presents, and they spent the 22nd together for their holiday celebration before he drove home the following day to see his family. Cassidy and Jake baked cookies, ate lots of appetizers, played multiple board games, drank copious amounts of beer, and spent a large amount of time naked in bed as Christmas music played in the background. The day was perfect.

Cassidy spent Christmas Eve at her parents' in the annual chaos of family, presents, food, and games before attending the candlelight service at her childhood church. The day brought comfort and joy to Cassidy. She always enjoyed her family's Christmas celebration, but this year, she realized how much it meant to her. For her gifts, she had noticed how much her brothers hated running errands, so she booked herself to help them out with multiple store and pick-up runs. Normally, Cassidy hated running errands too, but now she was thrilled to fill her time with something useful.

The holiday season came and went. Cassidy spent New Year's Eve watching the fireworks over the lake with Jake, Marissa, Brandon, and half the city. It almost felt normal, ringing in the start of 1988 with celebration, music, drinks, and fun. Cassidy knew this year would be better. It had to be.

Chapter 12

The first full week of 1988, the world seemed to go back to the usual routine. Schools were back in session, and everyone was back to work. Cassidy had a renewed sense of determination in her job search, telling herself that she would be hired by her 26th birthday -- even if that was only two and a half weeks away.

Jake had invited her over for dinner that night and Cassidy was thrilled to have an excuse to leave the apartment. She parked in front of his house just after six o'clock and knocked on the door. There was a long pause. She was about to knock again, but suddenly the white, wooden door swung open, revealing Jake wearing a red apron and looking a tad frazzled. Cassidy grinned at the sight of him.

"Hey," Jake said a little breathless.

"What is going on here?" Cassidy said unable to hide her smile at his apron.

"Cookin'! Come on in," Jake waved her inside. Cassidy gave him a quick peck as she passed him and stepped into the living room.

"What is on the menu, chef?" she asked, taking off her jacket, hat, gloves, and boots – it was bitter outside.

"Come into the kitchen and I'll show ya," Jake smiled as he hung her winter gear on the coat tree. Cassidy followed him to the brown and white kitchen in the back of the house. She was instantly struck by the amazing aroma that filled the air.

"Smells good in here!"

"Glad to hear that."

"Pasta?" Cassidy asked, looking at one of the pots on the stove.

"Yes, with homemade sauce, and garlic bread is in the oven." He smiled proudly.

"Homemade sauce?"

"Yes!"

"Like real tomatoes and spices and the lot?"

"Yes."

"If that's Ragu simmering…"

"It is not! Old family recipe. You can check my trash can if you don't believe me," Jake smirked proudly.

"Well, wow, wow, you are full of surprises," Cassidy chuckled to herself.

"Damn straight."

"Alright, what do you need help with?"

"I'm pretty much all set in here; everything should be done in a few minutes. But if you want to put silverware and napkins on the table, we'll plate in here."

"Can do," Cassidy said, kissing him on the cheek before getting to work as he continued to monitor the stove.

"Oh, what do you want to drink?" Jake called out as Cassidy finished folding the napkins under the forks.

"Hmm, wine feels appropriate, but I'll have whatever."

"I have a bottle of white in the fridge."

"I'll pour," Cassidy said happily. Within five minutes, Jake and Cassidy were seated at the square table in his dining room with plates of spaghetti and garlic bread covered in bolognese sauce.

"This is amazing," Cassidy said, popping another bite in her mouth. Jake grinned proudly.

"I'm glad you like it."

"Is this your mom's sauce recipe?" she asked, dipping the edge of her garlic bread in the sauce.

"My mom's mom's recipe, actually. But, yeah, that side of the family."

"Well, please tell her I love it... maybe it will win me a few points with her."

"I'll make sure to mention it," Jake chuckled. Cassidy picked up her wine glass.

"I know you think it's ridiculous, but I need all the Claire points I can get." Cassidy thought back to her meeting with Claire four months prior. It hadn't gone poorly, but wasn't spectacular, either. It never hurt to score some extra points.

"I'll see what I can do."

"So," Cassidy began, setting her wine back down after a long sip. "Is there any special reason you're feeding me this delicious meal?"

"Well," Jake hastily finished chewing. "Kind of."

"Really?"

"Well, I, um, wanted to share some news."

"Hmm?"

"I've been offered a job."

"What? Really?" Cassidy asked in a mix of shock and

excitement.

"Yeah, um, yep," Jake nodded, a small smile on his face.

"When did this happen?"

"Well, actually, just before Christmas, but I, I didn't want to say anything because... well, um,"

"Oh, Jake, no, you don't have to not be happy because I had a crappy month!" Cassidy said, reaching over and squeezing his hand. She wouldn't be able to forgive herself if he missed opportunities because of her.

"No, no, I've been given time to decide. Also, it let me think about it myself some," he explained

"Okay, okay, well, you've had time to think... I want to hear all about this job and what you're thinking. Come on, spill! Tell me everything!" Cassidy said excitedly.

"Another university has head hunted me... I never thought I would be someone that was actually head hunted." Jake used air quotes and Cassidy smiled.

"You are definitely someone who should be head hunted."

"Apparently. It's similar to my current role, but I'd be teaching more classes and still working with the baseball team. Even traveling more with them."

"Wow!"

"Yeah, I mean, it's a lot. I'd be a lot busier. Responsible for a lot more. Granted, the pay is... significantly more than I'm making now."

"This all sounds fantastic! I mean look at you, you're like bouncing with excitement," Cassidy said, reaching over to take his hand that was rattling his fork against his plate. He smiled at her.

"Umm, yeah..."

"What?"

"Northwestern."

"What?"

"Northwestern University is who reached out to me with the offer," Jake said, gulping loudly before pulling his hand out of hers and stuffing a forkful of spaghetti into his mouth. Cassidy paused. She could feel her mouth hanging open in surprise, and she quickly shut it.

"Like the Northwestern in Chicago?"

"Um, Evanston, but, yep," Jake replied with a full mouth.

"Where is Evanston?" Cassidy asked.

"Just north of Chicago."

"Chicago... in Illinois?" she clarified, despite fully knowing the answer.

"That's the one," Jake nodded. Cassidy looked down at her plate for a moment. She'd gone from excited to overwhelmed in a matter of seconds. The air felt heavy. She took a big gulp of wine.

"That's, that's a good school," she said lamely before digging back into her dinner. Her mind swirled as they ate in silence for a few minutes. Finally, Jake broke the quiet.

"Cassidy, I need you to say something. Please."

"What do you want me to say?" she asked as she swallowed hard on a large bite of garlic bread.

"What are you thinking?"

"What? What? Wah?" Cassidy stuttered. Jake tried to hide a smirk which annoyed her a little bit, if she was honest.

"Simple question."

"No! No, not a simple question!" Cassidy said, dropping her fork on the plate. The loud clank was oddly satisfying. "It's a loaded question. It's a multi-layer question. It's an overwhelming question!"

"Okay… then go through the layers."

"Ugh! Um, okay," she began, running her fingers through her hair roughly. "I… I'm excited that you were head hunted… that is honestly really cool. But I'm less excited that you're looking at a job three states away. However, if I object to that, it sounds like I don't want you to have this opportunity. Or that I'm harboring jealously about not having a job and you getting fucking head hunted by a prestigious university three states away," she huffed, leaning her head back for a long moment.

"Oh," Jake said. Cassidy's head snapped back down as she glared at him.

"I'm going to need a hell of a lot more than that, Sullivan."

"Well, honestly, I've been racking my brain trying to figure out how you were going to respond … you fell somewhere in the middle of my guesses." Jake shrugged before taking another bite of garlic bread. Cassidy bit down on her lip, hard.

"Jake, please don't make jokes right now. This is a big thing."

"I know it's a big thing. It's huge!"

"Okay… well, did you make a decision? Or are you waiting on me to make a decision, or what?" Cassidy asked, reaching for her wine again and downing the contents. She felt like her heart was in her throat.

"I don't have a final decision yet, but, well, depending on how this," he gestured between the two of them, "goes, I really want to drive out there and meet with some people and see what it's like in person before I commit to going or not."

"Oh," Cassidy let out a heavy breath. Her mind was racing. She was mildly annoyed that Jake was continuing to eat as if they were simply talking about the weather.

"Oh?" he asked, mouth full of pasta.

"You… you said if this goes well, if the telling me goes well. What did you think I would do? Throw a plate at the wall and storm out?"

"Honestly, it was one of the scenarios I played out, yes."

"Really?"

"If it helps, it was in the running for worst case scenario."

"In the running? What was my worst reaction in your head?"

"Death."

"You thought I'd die?"

"God no, I thought you'd kill me," Jake said plainly.

"You really thought I'd kill you?"

"How about I answer that when you aren't holding a fork," he suggested, the hint of a smirk on his face. Cassidy leaned over and punched his shoulder with her left fist.

"Ow," he chuckled. Cassidy smiled, despite herself.

"Jake," she cocked her head slightly.

"Cassidy, look, I love you, but you are, just the tiniest bit… intense, no, passionate," he said with a wince. Cassidy knew it was true, but whenever someone else pointed it out she felt her teeth clench in annoyance.

"Fine."

"So, yeah, I played out a few different options in my head."

"And made homemade sauce," she pointed out.

"And made homemade sauce," he nodded.

"That's annoyingly good."

"Good."

"And it's pacifying me slightly," Cassidy smirked as she twirled a forkful of spaghetti before popping it into her mouth. Jake grinned.

"Well, while you're slightly pacified, I wanted to ask you

if… you wanted to head out to Evanston -- Chicago -- with me for a few days?"

"Wait, when?"

"I was thinking of driving out on Saturday. We can look around on Sunday, get a feel for the area. I'd meet with some people at the university on Monday, then we'd head back home on Tuesday."

"Oh, wow!"

"I already took Monday and Tuesday as personal days at MU next week," he said. Cassidy swallowed hard. This suddenly felt like a lot again.

"Oh, I, um, I don't know if I--" she awkwardly stuttered.

"Because you're doing what?" Jake asked flatly. It was true she had nothing else to do with her time, but it was a low blow. Cassidy shot him an annoyed side-eye and she could see him grimace. "Sorry, that, that came out wrong."

"No, it came out right," she said, absentmindedly spinning her fork on her plate.

"Cassidy, I would really, really like it if you would go with me," Jake pleaded. Cassidy didn't answer for a long moment. She could feel Jake watching her.

"I guess," she let out a loud sigh. "I guess we never really have had a trip away together before, other than visiting family. But this would be just us."

"Yes, it would be just us," Jake said. While he kept his voice calm and steady, the look on his face was absolutely beaming. She couldn't help but smile back at him. He looked so happy.

"Look, I'm excited about an impromptu trip, but I'm also freaking out a bit because, well, this is more than just a trip. Like, what are we going to do? I've never even thought about moving out of state… at least not yet. And I don't know what this means for me or for us or… Do I really want to just follow a boy? I have a life here! I, I, I…" Cassidy frantically rambled. Jake scooted his chair slightly and reached over to grab her forearms to keep her still.

"Cassidy, Cassidy, Cassidy," he said until she stopped talking and just looked at him.

"What?" she asked, her voice low.

"You're getting ahead of yourself. I mean, we're not even there yet. What if I hate the city? What if I hate the school? Or my potential boss that's interviewing me? Nothing is set in stone. We're just going to go check the place out. We won't even have a decision made by Tuesday," he assured her, gently rubbing her inner arms with his thumbs. Cassidy took a slow, deep breath.

"I know, but I just want to be prepared. This is potentially huge and I'm kind of freaking out."

"I know you are," Jake said with a chuckle.

"Jacob!" Cassidy scolded before rolling her eyes.

"Ugh."

"What? You don't like Jacob?"

"I don't dislike it, but generally, if I was called Jacob, I was in trouble," he said.

"True, I mean I could… oh, my gosh!"

"What?"

"I was about to say I could call you by your full name, but I just realized I don't know your middle name. Oh, my gosh! I'm going away for a weekend with a guy I've been dating for like six months and I don't know his full name!" Cassidy gasped. She felt a mixture of amused and horrified by that. Jake, however, started to laugh, clearly he found it amusing.

"Is it really that bad?"

"I don't know, but feels strange."

"Okay, well, my middle name is Thomas. Are you happy now?" He raised an eyebrow playfully. Cassidy nodded.

"Jacob Thomas Sullivan," she said rhythmically. Jake nodded. "Thomas after your dad, right?"

"Yep," he confirmed. Cassidy knew little about his late father, Tom. Mostly just that he had worked all the time, had been a loud, angry man, and that he'd openly preferred Will to Jake. Tom and Jake's relationship had been frosty, at best, and Jake never seemed to miss the man much at all.

"Jacob Thomas Sullivan," Cassidy repeated.

"What's yours?"

"Lynne," she smiled.

"Ah, after your mother."

"Yep."

"Our parents aren't exactly creative, are they?" Jake teased, making Cassidy laugh.

"Well, not with either of us."

"True. You have a million brothers; they can't all have the middle name Arthur."

"Only Ben does," Cassidy told him. Jake looked surprised.

"That is not the brother I would have guessed!"

"Well, apparently my parents had agreed on Alex's first name but neither liked the alliteration of Alexander Arthur. I guess it got pushed to the side until Ben came and they wanted to get it in… especially after I got Lynne," Cassidy smiled.

"Okay, well, Cassidy Lynne Banker, can we finish our dinner and start talking about our upcoming trip?" he asked, sliding his hands down to hers and giving them a squeeze. Cassidy nodded.

"Sounds good."

Chapter 13

Cassidy slowly twirled the radio knob as the music turned to static once more. They were getting quite close to Chicago; city stations should be taking over soon. She couldn't wait. While the drive had been pleasant, the mid-song static as they drove out of range was getting old.

She and Jake had loaded up his truck and headed west before eight o'clock that morning. It was a seven-hour drive from Erie to Evanston, and their goal was to arrive by late afternoon. They had only stopped twice, once for lunch and fuel outside of Toledo, and again for a second fill up in Indiana. They were making good time and as much fun as they had been having, talking and laughing the whole trip, Cassidy was ready to be out of the truck.

"We should be close to the Illinois border," Cassidy commented after finding a station playing the Doobie Brothers and returning her attention to the map book in her lap.

"There is a sign up there." Jake pointed at a large green sign overhead that was just far enough they couldn't quite read yet.

The truck zoomed along with the growing traffic.

"Welcome to Chicago," Cassidy read as they approached. "Wow! We're in the city already?" she glanced down at her map once more.

"City limits, I'm guessing." Jake said. "But we still have to get to Evanston, which is on the north side of the city."

"But that shouldn't take that long, right?" Cassidy said. But as soon as the words were out of her mouth the red taillights of the cars in front of them started to glow, and their comfortable 70 mile-per-hour pace was down to a 30 mile-per-hour crawl.

"I think this will be the whole final hour of the trip," Jake hummed, sounding amused yet annoyed.

"Ugh. Our little city has not adequately prepared me for this big city traffic," she said, propping her right elbow on the window frame.

"It hasn't," Jake chuckled. "But I'm using my years of training from driving to Penn State games on Saturday mornings. Not a city, but those back roads don't handle the tailgating traffic."

"Didn't you live on campus?"

"When I went to school there, yes, but I grew up going to games and went to some after graduation. If you're not living there, it's a mess."

"Ahhh."

Despite the slow pace, heavy traffic, iffy merge attempts, and an absurd number of traffic lights, the drive through the city was kind of fun. Neither Cassidy nor Jake had ever been there before and they enjoyed seeing the skyscrapers, monuments, and general chaos that all big cities contain. Even with the grey winter sky and large piles of discolored snow everywhere, the city was still beautiful and captivating.

Almost a full hour after spotting the "Welcome to Chicago" sign, Jake pulled up to the large, red brick Hilton they had booked. It was only a couple of blocks from the University campus on the north edge of the city. After a slight struggle through an unpleasant underground parking garage, Jake and Cassidy took the elevator upstairs, checked in, and were given the keys to their room on the fourth floor.

"We're here!" Cassidy said happily with a breathy smile as she dropped her puffy coat, hat, and duffle bag on the bulky chair that was next to the king-sized bed.

"Yeah," Jake hummed, setting his bag and outer garments on the floor next to the chair as he took in his surroundings.

"Are you excited?" Cassidy asked, turning to face him as she rested her left knee on edge of the mattress.

"Yeah. Well, I mean, it feels surreal."

"Surreal? It's Chicago, not Paris!"

"I know, but … right now it's like a little vacation with my girlfriend. The whole reason we're here hasn't quite hit yet," he admitted with a shrug.

"Maybe that's good?"

"Ya think?"

"Maybe. I mean, you might be looking at the city more objectively… at least until your meetings on Monday," Cassidy suggested.

"Hmmm, not a bad thought."

"Do you know what else is a good thought?" she raised an eyebrow as she reached out for him. Jake chuckled as he walked forward and placed his hands on her hips.

"It's a very good plan, but I thought you wanted to be out of the car and stretch your legs."

"We are out of the car and my legs will get super stretched,"

121

she winked, wrapping her right arm around his shoulder and plunging the fingers of her left hand into his hair.

"You make excellent arguments."

"I know!" Cassidy grinned before pecking him on the lips.

"And I, personally, have never had sex in the state of Illinois before, so."

"So, that is totally a bucket list item."

"Absolutely! It's up there."

"Is this going to be our thing? We have to have sex in every new state we're in?" Cassidy asked with a laugh.

"I'm all for it," Jake said enthusiastically. "I'm not saying it has to happen the moment we cross the border, but definitely at some point during the stay."

"I love this plan." She kissed his chin. "Does that mean I need to make a checklist?"

"Oh, one hundred percent," he said, making Cassidy laugh. He kissed her on the cheek.

"I will definitely write one up when we get back to PA."

"Perfect," Jake whispered, kissing lower on her cheek. He was slowly making his way toward her mouth.

"Wait, wait!" Cassidy said, tapping his shoulders playfully.
"Hmm?"

"Do we have to spend the night or just time in the state? Because we drove through Ohio and Indiana today," she pointed out. Jake paused, looking entertained.

"I have not thought of the rules that clearly, but if you'd like, we can make a few extra stops on the drive back..."

"That's going to be a long ass trip home."

"The Indiana border is so close!"

"In distance, but we just sat in an hour of traffic to get away from that border. We'll have to be further into the state."

"Ah, real Indiana," Jake teased. Cassidy gave him a gentle shove.

"That's not what I meant."

"Or, if you suddenly want to be real efficient about all of this, we could find some place on the Indiana--Ohio border. It'll be two for one."

"That's cheating!"

"Says the girl who won't settle for Gary, Indiana," Jake said. Cassidy laughed loudly. She loved their playful banter.

"Shut up and kiss me," she said. Jake grinned before crashing his lips onto hers. The kiss deepened in seconds as her arms wrapped tightly around his shoulders and his arms circled her waist. They kissed passionately for almost a minute before Jake pushed her backwards, practically tackling her onto the bed. They broke apart laughing as they momentarily detangled and repositioned themselves on the bed so their heads were on the pillows. Cassidy snuggled close and kissed him.

"Excited to cross off Illinois?" Jake teased.

"Yes. Best welcome to a state ever!"

"Good."

"But after this, can we go out of the hotel and find someplace cool for dinner?"

"Oh, definitely," he nodded.

"This first, though?"

"This first," Jake grinned, pressing his lips to hers and rolling on top of her as her right leg wrapped around his waist.

The purple and grey sweatshirt selection was quite impressive. Cassidy perused the incredibly large university bookstore on campus. She was fairly certain her entire freshman dormitory at Edinboro University could fit in there. What a difference from a little state school to a massive university! Jake was currently in his interview and going into his third hour. She knew that he had a tour, multiple people to meet, and a lengthy list of questions he had prepared, so it was not going to be a quick event.

After their christening of Illinois on Saturday afternoon, Cassidy and Jake went out and walked around the few city blocks surrounding their hotel. Despite being bundled and used to cold, snowy weather, the Chicago winter air felt piercing. They found a Korean restaurant and had an amazing dinner – the first time either of them had tried Korean food. It definitely wouldn't be the last.

Sunday was a full day of exploration. After chickening out with attempting to navigate the subway, they took a taxi down to the heart of Chicago and spent the day visiting museums, the riverwalk, and even the aquarium. They had deep dish pizza for lunch, snacked on Garrett Popcorn, and went to a beautiful Mediterranean restaurant for dinner where Cassidy had lamb stew and Jake tried a grilled shrimp kebab. Both were delicious. After dinner they found a brewery where they drank a couple of beers as they chatted, relaxed, and had the most delightful people watching. Too tipsy to attempt to navigate, they took the long cab ride back north and stumbled into their hotel room a few minutes after midnight.

Grabbing coffee and a bagel for breakfast on Monday morning, Jake and Cassidy walked to Northwestern to explore the campus. It was lightly snowing, and it made the historic campus look almost magical. The students were all back from break and there was a fun atmosphere. Jake and Cassidy wandered aimlessly for a couple of hours, exploring buildings and snow covered sports fields, before grabbing a quick lunch at a sub shop. Then Jake headed to his interview. Cassidy gave him a quick good luck kiss and waved him off.

She went back to the hotel for a nap and a chance to warm up a bit. Once rested and freshened up, Cassidy returned to campus and started her exploration of the university bookstore, which honestly, she could have been happily lost in for hours.

Cassidy unfolded one of the sweatshirts and held it up to examine it. Should she buy one? Even just as a souvenir? This trip had been one of the best of her entire life. She wanted to remember it forever. She no longer knew what she wanted from Jake's interview. A few days ago, she had wanted it to fail, but she thought that might be changing. She quickly refolded the shirt and returned it to the shelf. Perhaps a "Chicago" refrigerator magnet from one of the cheesy tourist shops would suffice.

She had just made it to the overwhelming selection of hats when she heard her name called. Jake was walking quickly toward her with a big grin on his face. It must have gone well. Cassidy couldn't decide if she should cheer or just start crying. Possibly both.

"Hey!" he said, slinging his arm around her shoulder.

"Hi, how did it go?"

"Come on, let's get out of here. I'll tell you all about it."

"Okay, but where are we going?" Cassidy asked as she let him lead her out of the large store and back to the cold outdoors. She involuntarily bristled as the wind hit her in the face.

"Let's go get something to eat."

"It's only three-thirty," she pointed out with a giggle.

"We can get a drink and a snack, just somewhere inside where we can sit."

"Inside sounds great!" Cassidy agreed. They both zipped up their coats as far as they could go and walked as closely as they could, Jake with his arm around her shoulders, and Cassidy had her left arm around his back. It may have looked romantic, but honestly, they were both just trying to keep warm.

It was a very brisk twenty-minute walk to get off campus and to a bar and grill they had passed a few times previously. It was warm and rustic looking. The restaurant was over half full. A small TV over the bar showed sports analysts recounting last night's Blackhawks game. Cassidy and Jake were seated at a small wooden booth. They quickly ordered a beer each and a large plate of fries to share.

"Well? Are you going to tell me how it went?" Cassidy asked with a smile. Jake grinned back.

"It went… perfect," he breathed.

"Perfect?"

"Yes! Everyone was great. They answered every single one of my questions. I got a tour of the math department, met some of the heads. Then we went over to the athletic department and met the staff there for the baseball team. They have a huge staff. About three times the number of people at Mercyhurst."

"It's a significantly bigger school."

"Yeah. I just… I don't know, it went better than I could have hoped," he said. He looked slightly dazed. Cassidy willed herself not to burst into tears.

"Did you sign anything?"

126

"No, not yet. I have a week to decide. They told me to take a few days and think about it. They don't want to put in all the effort of bringing me on just for me to panic, change my mind and quit."

"Smart," she nodded. They were interrupted by their waitress returning to the table.

"Here you go," she set two full glasses of beer on the table. "And those fries will be out in a minute."

"Thanks," Jake smiled at her.

"Did they talk about salary? What about moving time? When would you start -- if you take the job? What about benefits? Where would you live?"

"Cassidy," Jake said calmly, reaching over and taking her hand in his. "This is a lot, I know."

"It is a lot, and you need to go over all the details," she said, picking up her glass and taking a large gulp.

"Yes, I know, and I asked a lot of questions. I thought they would think it was ridiculous, but they seemed to enjoy it."

"Okay."

"Do you want me to go over it all?"

"Obviously! We're not here to discuss anything else," Cassidy pointed out. She knew her words came out sassier than she intended.

"Fair," he smiled.

"Run it down: the good, the bad, the ugly," she said, pulling her hand out of his as she gestured. Jake excitedly pulled a yellow notepad out of his bag.

"Alright," he began, but was interrupted by another appearance by their waitress.

"Piping hot, here you go!" she said cheerily as she set down a massive basket of crispy fries and a bottle of ketchup. They sure did look delicious. Cassidy wasted no time in squeezing a dollop of ketchup out in the corner of the basket as Jake once again thanked the waitress and she disappeared.

"You were saying," Cassidy prompted, popping a fry in her mouth.

"Okay, well, the salary is great – a lot more than my current one."

"Chicago … um, Evanston, is a lot more expensive than Erie."

"I know."

"Of course, you've done the math," Cassidy smirked as she ate another fry.

"I have. But the money is good, even for out here. Benefits and days off are almost identical to what I have now. Definitely more responsibilities. I mean, it will be the same with the baseball team, but it is a much bigger program with a lot of travel."

"Do you want to do more travel?"

"I think so. It would be a cool way to see more of the country," Jake said as he reached for a few fries.

"True."

"I'd be teaching three classes."

"All stats?"

"Yes. One intro class, which they said would be mostly freshman and sophomores, and then two upper-level ones."

"What do you think about that?"

"I like the idea of teaching more, though honestly I'm not thrilled about getting freshman."

"I'm sure they won't be that bad."

"Second semester won't be, but first semester... yes. The incoming freshman that come for baseball camp each summer are like squirrels." Jake groaned making Cassidy chuckle.

"Eh, a bunch will probably drop the class in the first month, then you'll be left with the kids that want to be there."

"Yeah."

"And you like teaching the higher-level stuff."

"I really do."

"And you'll have two of those."

"Yeah."

"How often are the classes?" Cassidy asked.

"Intro is a two-hour class twice a week. Apparently, it's usually Tuesdays and Thursdays, but some semesters it can differ. And both upper levels are ninety minutes each, three days a week."

"So you'll have two classes on Monday, Wednesdays, and Fridays and one on Tuesdays and Thursdays? Sounds nice."

"I think one of the uppers is Monday, Tuesday, Thursday, but yeah, I should have a full week." Jake took a sip of his beer.

"You like the school, you like the team, what about housing? Moving? When do you have to start?"

"I would just find a local apartment to rent. As for moving," Jake checked his notes, "they offered to pay for a moving truck."

"How would you get your truck here?"

"I'd either tow it, or maybe Will can drive out with me and then fly home."

"Okay." Cassidy took a large gulp for her glass. This was feeling very real.

"But I'm not leaving next week," he assured her cheerily.

"When would you leave?"

"Summer. Well, just before."

"Summer?"

"I'd be shadowing part of the summer semester, and then helping out with the baseball camps and clinics, and then the fall semester starts."

"So, you'd hit the ground running."

"Kind of. Ideally, I'd like to have a week to move in and get my bearings, but shadowing shouldn't be too taxing," he explained as he grabbed for more fries. Cassidy watched him. He was excited. She could see the wheels turning in his head as he planned this next adventure. She should be happy for him. She should be excited with him. But his excitement was over four hundred miles from her entire world. Hell, it was in a different time zone. Cassidy didn't know what to feel or to say. She just hurt.

"Okay," she breathed.

"Cassidy, come on, I need you to tell me what you think," Jake urged before taking another drink.

"I think you've already made up your mind."

"I'm running on adrenaline right now. They told me to take the week to decide and that's what I'm going to do, but I would like some feedback."

"I…" Cassidy paused, twirling a fry between her fingers. "I think it's perfect."

"Except you sound like you would rather be at the dentist."

"Well, I'm frustrated."

"I can tell."

"Jake, this is serious." Cassidy shot him a look.

"No, no, I know it is," he held up his hands in defense.

"This is all perfect. The perfect job, the perfect everything. Except for the fact that it's in a different state and I have no idea what the hell that means for us… For me, if I'm being honest." She swallowed hard.

"You switched from 'us' to 'me.'"

"I, I, I, ugh, how am I supposed to phrase this…?"

"Look, we're still talking about all of this. I don't want anything decided tonight. But if I do take this job… I would really like you to come with me."

"Come with you," Cassidy repeated slowly.

"We can start our own life here."

"We have a life!"

"We do, but we can start something for us, a new path, new opportunities. We'll just figure it all out," he said adamantly.

"Figure it all out. On our own. In a strange city. Hours away from our friends and family."

"Yes. It's almost romantic," Jake smiled.

"It's scary as hell."

"That adds to it all. Think about the pilgrims! They traveled across the ocean for a new adventure and life together! Romantic!"

"Like, half of them died in the first year."

"And half didn't."

"I don't like this fifty-fifty-chance-we-may-die analogy." Cassidy made a face.

"Okay, okay. I'm just saying, this is something I want to really discuss this over the next few days," Jake said earnestly.

"Okay," Cassidy let out a deep breath. "We'll discuss it. Really lay it all out."

"Great, thank you."

"I mean, we do have a seven hour drive tomorrow."

"We do! With two stops. Maybe more if we dip over the Michigan border. It's only like, a five-mile detour," Jake winked. Cassidy rolled her eyes.

"Don't push your luck, Sullivan."

"Eh, we'll see."

"Okay… but we still have all evening here. Can we table the job talk and enjoy our last night in the city?" she asked.

"I would love nothing more," Jake said. He raised his glass. Cassidy held hers up and clinked it against his. They both took a long drink. She was excited to enjoy a final night downtown before reality came crashing back in.

Chapter 14

The microwave beeped and the smell of popcorn filled the air. Cassidy poured the contents of the hot bag into a large white bowl and carried it into the living room.

"Ah, yay," Marissa said happily, reaching up for the bowl as Cassidy walked by to take her seat on the other end of the couch. Cassidy playfully pulled the bowl out of Marissa's grasp before setting it on the couch between them and they both dug in.

Cassidy had arrived back home from Evanston less than an hour ago. Marissa was just finishing dinner when Cassidy walked back into the apartment. After a quick hello, Cassidy took a much-needed shower and changed into her PJs. Now the girls were both comfy and settled on the couch. Marissa was anxious for her promised debrief of the trip.

"Alright," Marissa said as she chomped on a mouthful of popcorn. "What happened on the trip?"

"A lot," Cassidy said honestly.

"I need more than that."

"It was fantastic!"

"Your face is not relaying that."

"Because… I think Jake is taking the job," Cassidy sighed.

"He didn't have to decide there?" Marissa asked.

"No. They're giving him until Friday."

"That's nice."

"Yes, it is. They are very nice, the school is very nice, the city is very nice," Cassidy said glumly.

"Okay, again, your words and face don't match," Marissa pointed out. She tossed a kernel of popcorn at Cassidy and she gave a small chuckle.

"I'm feeling lots of things at once."

"I can tell."

"The trip was wonderful. Honestly, one of my favorites ever. Jake and I had so much fun. I loved it."

"I'm glad," Marissa smiled.

"And the interview went well. Jake loves the job."

"He's taking it?"

"He really wants to."

"Okay… so what does that —?"

"I'm still not sure what that means for me or us," Cassidy interrupted.

"Hmmm."

"We talked about it a lot."

"About the job?"

"About it all. I mean, it was a long car ride."

"Yeah, you got back later than I would have thought."

"Well… we made a few stops," Cassidy blushed. Marissa watched her for a moment.

"Oh, gah, you had car sex, didn't you? Ugh, and on the interstate?!"

"Not car sex per se…"

"Please don't tell me it was gross gas station sex?"

"Ew, no!"

"But you're not going to tell me where?"

"You won't be happy," Cassidy admitted in a low chuckle as Marissa gave a whine and covered her face dramatically.

"Ugh! Okay, perverted stops aside, you said you talked?"

"Yeah. Yeah, we did," Cassidy nodded.

"And?"

"And he's highly, highly considering taking the offer. I mean, he's talking like he's thinking about it, but I know he's decided. He wants this. He needs this. I mean, it's perfect for him."

"Mmmm," Marissa hummed as she scrunched up her nose.

"What?"

"No, no. Continue."

"You made a face like it's not a good job for him."

"I'm sure the job is great, but you're talking like it's the only perfect thing for him."

"Are you alluding to me?"

"A bit."

"Well, the job is perfect, and... Well, he wants me to go with him," Cassidy bit her lip. Marissa just stared at her.

"Move to Chicago?"

"Yeah."

"What would you do there?"

"I would have to find a job."

"So, just start over?"

"Well, it's not like I have a job here..." Cassidy said. Marissa winced.

"Shit."

"Yeah, shit." Both girls sighed in defeat. A long, heavy

pause filled the air.

"Well," Marissa began slowly. "What would you be saying if you still had your job here?"

"But I don't."

"I know that, but that is almost like pushing your hand… so, what if this happened and you and Jake had your trip and all that is the same, but you had a job here that you would need to quit?"

"Umm…"

"Just think about it."

"I don't know how to answer that."

"Would it make a difference in your decision or trepidation?"

"I want Jake to be happy."

"I get that."

"Either way, I'd have to go find a job there," Cassidy said flatly as she reached forward and grabbed a firm fistful of popcorn. It crunched slightly in her hand.

"I know."

"Marissa, what do you want me to say? I'm stressed. This sucks. No matter what I choose, I'm going to be sad."

"I know."

"Stop saying that," Cassidy snapped. Marissa sighed.

"Look, I don't want you to move. I'm going to be selfish and I'm not ready for us to move apart."

"Clearly, I'm not either."

"But," Marissa swallowed, "you've been happier with Jake than I've ever seen you."

"So, you're saying I should go?"

"No."

"So, I should stay?"

"No."

"Well, those are my two options," Cassidy pointed out. They shared a sad smile.

"When do you have to tell him by?"

"He has until Friday to make his decision, but I'm thinking he's going to call on Thursday."

"So, two days?"

"I mean, he won't move for a few months, but I'd definitely need to make a decision before he finds an apartment," Cassidy shrugged.

"What about your family?"

"They'll stay here," Cassidy quipped. Marissa rolled her eyes.

"I mean are you going to make the decision with them?"

"No. I like to know what I want before I get them involved."

"Fair," Marissa chuckled.

"I don't how I'd even tell them… either way."

"Why?"

"It's going to be a mess. I leave, they'll be sad; I stay, they'll miss Jake."

"You think Jake is part of their preference now?" Marissa smirked.

"They loved him. I think they like him more than me sometimes!"

"I wouldn't go that far."

"Okay, just Matty," Cassidy teased. Her heart felt tighter thinking about her family. What the hell was she going to do? The two friends sat in a comfortable, sad silence for a long minute.

"What do you need from me?" Marissa asked.

"Make the decision for me?" Cassidy asked with a grimace.

"I can't do that," Marissa said sadly.

Cassidy looked surprised. "What? I would have expected you to tell me I have to stay!"

"Dunno," Marissa replied lamely.

"Oh, my gosh."

"I don't want you to go, but I don't want you to mope around here for a year after he leaves, either!"

"You think I'll mope for a year?"

"You did after Kevin dumped you."

"That was a low blow," Cassidy bit her tongue.

"I'm sorry."

"I know."

"Cassidy… I can't decide for you. But you should think one year from now, what will you be doing? What will life be like, either way? You have to make your choice based on where you want to be for your twenty-seventh birthday."

"Hmmm."

"And do me a favor? Don't make a decision in two days."

"So, three or four?" Cassidy joked.

"Yes, that's exactly what I meant," Marissa replied sarcastically.

"I know what you meant."

"Just, keep me in the loop."

"Definitely."

"Do you want to watch some TV?" Marissa asked, repositioning herself slightly.

"Yeah, sure. I could use a distraction," Cassidy said as Marissa grabbed the remote.

"It's almost nine – Moonlighting will be starting soon."

"Bruce Willis will help," Cassidy smirked as Marissa flipped to the channel. Despite the distraction, her mind continued to swirl. She had no idea what she was going to do.

Chapter 15

Jake accepted the job at Northwestern Thursday morning. She'd known he would. It was a fantastic opportunity for him. However, she still had not made a decision for herself. He took her out on Friday in a joint celebration – his new job and her birthday on the nineteenth, which was that Saturday. Despite the daunting changes on the horizon, the night was perfect. Jake took them to the Chinese restaurant where they had had their first date, followed by the movies to see Good Morning, Vietnam. It had come out at Christmas, but neither had had a chance to see it yet. The night was perfectly topped off by Jake spending the night at Cassidy's apartment. They didn't get to sleep until the wee hours of the morning.

Saturday morning, Cassidy's birthday started the same way it had every year since her sophomore year of college when she turned twenty – Marissa waking her up with a loud rendition of "Happy Birthday" as she brought her a chocolate eclair in bed and concluded her song with party popper of exploding confetti on her comforter. It was a tradition that made Cassidy laugh each year -- and one that startled the hell out of Jake. He was extraordinarily grateful that he'd decided to put his boxers back on before falling asleep. Marissa and a plate of doughnuts were suddenly on the bed with them as pink and green confetti showered over their heads.

Once Jake's heart rate had returned to normal, they finished their breakfast treats, cleaned up, got ready for the day. The three enjoyed a peaceful and happy morning together before Jake left shortly after lunch.

That afternoon Cassidy drove to her parents' house for a birthday dinner with the family for her and Eric. Cassidy honestly couldn't remember the last time she'd celebrated on her actual birthday with her family. Probably her eighteenth birthday in senior year of high school. That felt like a lifetime ago.

"Happy birthday!" Lynne called loudly, opening the front door the moment Cassidy stepped onto the porch.

"Thanks, mom," Cassidy said, hugging her.

"Twenty-six. I can't believe it!" Lynne said, pulling Cassidy inside.

"Oh, it smells good in here," Cassidy commented as the scent of the kitchen hit her nose.

"Why thank you – pot roast."

"Mmm."

"It should be ready in an hour," Lynne smiled.

"Ahh! You're here! Happy birthday!" Ellie gushed, bounding down the stairs. Eric slowly trailed behind her.

"Thanks!" Cassidy grinned at her almost sister-in-law before Ellie crashed into her with a big hug.

"It's fun having two people to celebrate!" Ellie said, pulling back.

"Oh, yes, yes," Cassidy said, looking over at her twin who was now standing on the bottom step behind Ellie. "Happy Birthday!"

"Happy Birthday," he nodded. The two shared a smirk.

"Where's Jake?" Ellie asked curiously.

"Oh!" Cassidy paused in surprise.

"You didn't dump him already, did you?" Eric groaned.

"Wait, you broke up?" Ellie asked sadly.

"What?" Cassidy tried to interject.

"You finally date someone good, but give him the heave," Eric said with a sigh.

"Guys, guys, no! I didn't dump Jake. We're great. I just didn't realize he was invited, or think to ask," Cassidy frantically clarified.

"Oh, good," Ellie smiled.

"Yes, good," Lynne agreed looking relieved before turning back into the kitchen.

"Hey," Cassidy reached over and pushed Eric's arm. "Did you really not like any of my boyfriends before?" she asked curiously.

"No. All douchebags," he replied flatly. Ellie let out a snort but quickly tried to hold her reaction back after seeing Cassidy's annoyed look at Eric. She was clearly torn on which twin she wanted to support in the moment.

"What about Mike Karlin from down the street? We all used to play together as kids."

"That's called geographical convenience – it's how kid friendships work."

"You never liked him?"

"No, he was annoying. And he got progressively more annoying for that, what, ten days you dated him in ninth

141

grade," Eric pointed out.

"We dated for like two months," Cassidy corrected.

"My deepest apologies to that love story." He rolled his eyes.

"Oh, would you like me to give dear Ellie the run-down of all the winners you dated?" Cassidy challenged.

"We've already had that discussion and she was unfazed," Eric smirked.

"Makes sense. Lot of low cards in that hand. She has no competition," Cassidy sassed before turning to Ellie. "And I mean that with love, Ellie. You're fantastic and definitely a high card. Truly exceeded the low bar your predecessors set."

"Thanks, I think?" Ellie chuckled.

"It's a compliment," Cassidy assured her with a smile.

A loud crash from outside startled the three. They shared a quick look before pulling open the front door and clamoring out onto the porch.

"Oh my God," Eric said in a low, mildly entertained voice. There, at the end of the driveway were both Matty and Ben's cars. Matty's was horizontal across the entrance of the drive while Ben's front bumper was resting against the mailbox, which was now at a forty-five degree angle. The red pick-up flag on the side had fallen off and was sticking up right out of the snow.

"What the hell happened?" Art boomed as he pushed around the twins and Ellie and stomped off the porch. Both Matty and Ben hopped out of their cars, yelling and pointing fingers.

"I was just coming down the street and he's up my ass!" Matty complained to Art.

"We're going to the same place!" Ben held his arms out in annoyance.

142

"Trying not to get hit by speed racer, here, I turned in but hit ice," Matty grumbled.

"You know you're not supposed to hit your breaks on ice. That's why you spun," Ben pointed out obnoxiously.

"Do I want to go out there?" Lynne called from the kitchen, the front door still wide open.

"No," Cassidy, Eric, and Ellie replied in unison.

"Good," Lynne replied, her focus on the meal.

"And what about you?" Art asked his youngest as he had reached the end of the driveway.

"I was trying to get in and Matty starts spinning, so I had to get out of the way."

"I wouldn't have spun if you weren't an idiot!" Matty argued.

"Get out of the way into the mailbox?" Art pointed at the strained post.

"Would you rather I hit Matty?"

"A little."

"What?!" Matty asked in a loud squeak.

"You'd be fine," Art said nonchalantly, his focus and annoyance still on his youngest.

"I could be dead," Matty argued.

"Yeah, dad! Matty could be dead," Ben said, attempting to argue his case.

"Are you going to fix this?" Art asked, pointing at the tilted pole once more.

"Not immediately," Ben said.

"Why not?"

"Because there's like, two feet of snow!" Ben used his boot to kick a clump in the air.

"There's always snow! It's winter!" Art said angrily.

"Which is why you should know how to drive in it," Matty chimed in. Ben flipped him off. Art ignored the gesture.

"How are we supposed to get our mail?" he asked.

"The box is still here, it'll work just fine," Ben said as he dramatically opened and closed the little door on the mailbox to prove his point.

"Wow," Cassidy said in a low voice. A giant smile grew on her face. Eric shared a similar expression.

"I know. This is the best birthday present ever," he said.

"They were so thoughtful this year." Cassidy and Eric shared a look before bursting into laughter. Ellie stood on the other side of Eric looking absolutely mesmerized as she watched her future in-laws arguing about the crooked mailbox's workability. Cassidy was laughing so hard she didn't hear what made her father scream, "that is not what that means!" but she decided it was best to leave the scene. She really wanted to warm up indoors.

Eric and Ellie followed her inside and closed the front door behind them.

"Hey mom, um, don't look outside," Eric said, his laughter slowly dying out as he walked into the kitchen with Ellie in tow.

"Ugh, too late." Lynne rolled her eyes and continued chopping. Cassidy joined them in the kitchen as soon as she finished shedding her winter gear.

It was a few more minutes before Art, Matty, and Ben all came inside. Cassidy noticed that Matty's left cheek looked especially red. When she asked if he was okay Matty explained that Ben threw a snowball at him and called him a few choice words in the process. Lynne quickly put the two on a few kitchen chores. Cassidy, Eric, and Ellie happily sat

144

at the breakfast nook in the back of the kitchen and Art huffed off to his study.

Alex arrived thirty minutes later and got a spatula lobbed at him by Ben when his opening question was, "What happened to the mailbox?"

The family birthday celebration went quite smoothly after the initial kerfuffle. Everyone shared memories of the twins, and only a few were horribly embarrassing for Cassidy, which she actually felt was a pretty good ratio. Dinner was absolutely delicious, followed by the birthday cakes – yellow cake with chocolate frosting for Cassidy and chocolate cake with peanut butter frosting for Eric. Lynne always made sure each of them felt special on their birthday and they always had specially catered treats. The rest of the family enjoyed the tradition of getting two slices of cake. Ben prided himself on managing to down four slices every year!

After dinner, presents, and three rounds of Pictionary, the evening was winding down. Cassidy went to the kitchen to help her mom clean up while the boys and Ellie went through one of the old photo albums, laughing loudly.

"Here you go, I think this is everything from the table," Cassidy said as she carried a large stack of plates into the kitchen and set them on the island.

"Thank you, darling, but you don't have to help. It is your birthday, remember," Lynne smiled.

"I appreciate that, but this honestly is preferable to the old vacation photo album."

"Ah, the one with our trip down to the Carolinas?"

145

"How did you know?"

"Because you always get very upset when we go through that one." Lynne failed to suppress her chuckle.

"That's because they tell the same damn stories over and over," Cassidy grumbled.

"Memories don't really come with new stories."

"I know that."

"And I know that you're overly sensitive about them teasing you for throwing up at that restaurant when we stopped for lunch," Lynne acknowledged.

"I'm not overly sensitive; they are jerks! And--"

"Cassidy," Lynne said in a light, chiding tone.

"I'm not the bad guy here."

"I didn't say that; I just think you need to let this one go. You threw up -- everyone throws up."

"I didn't feel well from the windy roads and they put us at the table right next to the kitchen and the smoking section. It turned my stomach and I couldn't stop it." Cassidy let out a loud sigh.

"I understand, dear."

"I just was really sick. I don't need them mocking me spewing."

"You hit four tables and one of the waiters."

"It was so embarrassing. They made me stand off to the side and everyone there stared at me," Cassidy said, flinching at the memory.

"Your father paid for the three other tables' meals," Lynne said.

"I don't understand why we couldn't have just left?"

"I brought you in a change of clothes. And frankly, the staff worked so hard, we felt we had to stay. We tipped, like, forty percent," Lynne said, collecting the plates from the island and bringing them over to the sink.

"Mom," Cassidy groaned.

"You brought it up," Lynne shrugged as she poured more dish soap in the sink.

"Fine."

"So," Lynne began after a moment of silence. "Any luck on the job search?"

"Um…"

"Um?" Lynne looked over at her daughter with a raised eyebrow.

"Jake got a new job," Cassidy said.

"I didn't know he was looking."

"He wasn't."

"Oh… well, can you take his old job?" Lynne asked playfully. Cassidy paused for a moment. She'd never considered that angle before. She wasn't a statistician, but she was good at math and picked things up easily. Cassidy shook the idea out of her head.

"No."

"Is he still at Mercyhurst?"

"Um," Cassidy nervously tapped her fingers on the countertop.

"Cassidy Lynne Banker, are you pregnant?" Lynne asked in alarm.

"What? No! Mom!"

"You're acting weird, I just thought you were stalling on telling me something big."

"I'm not pregnant, mom."

"Okay," Lynne hummed as she scrubbed a spot on one of the dishes.

"But it is big…" Cassidy blurted out.

"Yeah?" Lynne set the plate down and shut off the water.

"Jake got a job at Northwestern University… outside of Chicago."

"Wow, that's very impressive!" Lynne said. Cassidy gave her a strange look.

"I mean, yeah, it is."

"But that's not the point," Lynne said knowingly.

"No, it's not."

"Is he taking the job?"

"Yes."

"And?"

"And what?" Cassidy asked.

"There are a lot of 'whats' there…"

"I know!" Cassidy whined.

"Cassidy, come here, talk to me," Lynne said as she dried her hands on the dishtowel. Cassidy walked around to her side of the island and rested her back along the edge of the counter.

"I don't know what to do, mom."

"What are your options?"

"Options make this sound clinical. This is my life!" Cassidy let out a loud breath.

"Lives have options, too."

"Yeah."

"So?"

"So… I like Jake a lot."

"I know," Lynne smiled.

"Jake wants to go. Well, he is going. I mean, it's a really good job. We went out to visit the other week. It was great. But I just… don't know. I mean, he would love me to go with him, but what the heck am I going to do there?"

"Find a job," Lynne suggested.

"You sound like Jake."

"Hmmm."

"I'm not… well, okay. I am afraid to start over in a new city, but I don't have a job there… or here."

"Right."

"Mom, I don't want to be the girl that follows a boy. And just have nothing of my own."

"I wouldn't want you to have nothing of your own. I may have waited for your father to finish college so we could marry, but I took my school nurse certification course and started working."

"I know!"

"Cassidy, you are very smart. You can find a job."

"Clearly I haven't proven that lately." Cassidy made a face.

"You were let go right before the holidays, it was really horrible timing," Lynne said.

"Are you wanting me to go?" Cassidy asked curiously.

"Well, obviously, I love having you close. I want you to find a job and be happy and have a good life. Jake makes you happier than I've ever seen you."

"Oh."

"Cassidy, I will support you. If you find a job you love here, and want to live your life in Pennsylvania, that's fantastic! But if you find a job you love somewhere else, I won't be angry with you."

"I appreciate that."

"You also don't need to decide this exact second."

"I kind of do… Jake leaves before the summer."

"Wow."

"Yeah."

"That's still many months away."

"I don't know what to do," Cassidy gulped loudly. Lynne reached over and rubbed her shoulders.

"You'll figure it out. You're twenty-six now. A full adult! You make your own choices."

"You're not going to tell me what to do?"

"You'll just do the opposite," Lynne smirked.

"Very funny, mom."

"Cassidy, make the decision that's right for you. Not for me, or your dad, or Jake, or Marissa. You," Lynne said firmly. Cassidy nodded.

"Thanks."

"But I will say, no matter what -- and you know I love Jake -- make sure you have something for you. Other than Jake."

"Yeah."

"I love your father, and we rely on each other for love and support. That's what marriage is. However, we have shared friends and separate ones. We have our separate jobs, we have our own interests. That doesn't mean we don't spend the majority of our time together or don't love one another more than life itself. But I don't want you to be solely dependent on Jake for every single aspect of your life."

"No, I'd kill him," Cassidy said. Lynne chuckled and nodded knowingly. "That's why I don't want to just follow a boy."

"I don't want you to just follow a boy. But I don't want you to disregard the boy because he has opened up a new path," Lynne said.

"Thanks, mom."

"Anytime."

"One more thing?"

"Yes?" Lynne asked.

"Don't tell dad yet... please?" Cassidy asked. Lynne hesitated for a moment before she let out a sigh.

"Fine, but you should tell him sooner rather than later. He's going to need time to process it. If you move, he'll be sad, and if you and Jake break up, he'll be sad."

"Dad likes Jake?"

"Very much. I'm going to get an earful tonight that he wasn't here."

"I'll make sure to coordinate a playdate for them, soon," Cassidy teased. Lynne laughed before kissing her daughter on the cheek.

"Alright, now go join your brothers, or I'll make you wash dishes on your birthday."

"Thanks, mom," Cassidy smiled before turning and heading out of the kitchen to join her father, brothers, and Ellie. She felt lighter after talking to her mom. This had been a great birthday.

Chapter 16

The day was finally here. Saturday, February 6, 1988. Eric and Ellie's wedding. It was just below freezing and hadn't snowed for two days. By all accounts, the weather was downright pleasant for an Erie winter.

Cassidy was sitting in the passenger's seat of Laura's car as they drove through the city to the church on the far east side of Erie. The rest of the Banker family had been at the church before lunch for the full day of prep.

Both Cassidy and Laura had attended the rehearsal and dinner the evening before. There were three run-throughs, and still bumps. Cassidy and Laura watched in amusement from one of the side pews. Being left out of the wedding party had turned into quite a blessing as last week Cassidy listened to the saga of the bachelorette party from the previous month. While Ellie had extended her an invitation, her sister Kara firmly insisted that everything had been perfectly planned out for just the six of them, and that Cassidy being odd number seven would mess things up. Honestly, Cassidy had been thrilled to be brutally uninvited by Kara. The last thing she needed to do was pay too much for drinks, listen to the inside jokes of Ellie and her friends, and listen to Ellie talk about sex with her brother, ugh. Most importantly, Cassidy did not need to get into a fight and give Kara a black eye. Cassidy had a short fuse on a good day, and her almost sister-in-law's older sister drove her crazy. Lynne would never forgive her if she got into a brawl with the wedding party. However, Matty would quickly deem her his favorite sibling had it happened.

But all of those events had passed. It was wedding day. The big day!

After making amends with Eric, and her mother last summer, Cassidy had dropped her crusade for a personal invitation to the wedding. She even avoided asking for a plus one. She was determined to prove that she could be supportive and simply enjoy her brother's wedding without bringing any attention to herself. Not to mention with all of Alex's groomsman duties, she would get plenty of time to hang out with Laura one on one. Something she truly enjoyed.

"Are you excited?" Laura asked as they idled at a red light.

"Um, I guess, yeah," Cassidy shrugged with a smile.

"Okay," Laura chuckled.

"I'm not mad! Honestly, I'm happy. And really excited to see Ellie's dress."

"Did she tell you anything about it?"

"I believe the term she used was poofy," Cassidy said.

Laura hummed as she accelerated once more.

"Also, Matty bet me five bucks that at least one person was going to trip down the aisle," Cassidy smirked.

"What? Last night he bet Alex ten dollars that Eric was going to fumble his lines."

"Oh jeez… guess he's covering every odd. I wonder how many bets he's made in total?" Cassidy thought out loud.

"He'll forget all about it," Laura snorted. Cassidy frantically shook her head.

"No, Matty is very alert when money is involved. And surprisingly organized. I can only imagine that he has a whole ledger in a black book somewhere."

"Do you want to make a bet on how much he's going to make by tonight?" Laura teased.

"No thanks, Matty would demand a cut," Cassidy chuckled as they turned into the narrow driveway to the church. The church was a large, dark red brick building that looked like it had been there for a century. The large, snow-covered steeple must have been almost one hundred feet in the sky. The white snow glistened in the sun. Cassidy smiled up at it as she stepped out of the car before grabbing her purse and small tote bag with her dressy heels. She was wearing her snow boots until she got inside – the last thing she needed to do was wipe out in the parking lot or on the stairs into the church. Both Cassidy and Laura hurried into the warmth of the church.

"Oh, you're here!" Lynne gushed as the girls removed their bulky coats and boots in the narthex. Cassidy appreciated the spacious coat wall with benches for changing shoes.

"Hi mom," Cassidy said with a smile. Her mother looked beautiful. Her short, blonde hair had been curled and she was in a long, grey dress and black heels.

"Oh, don't you two look nice," Lynne said, coming to hug both Cassidy and Laura. Cassidy was in a long, petal pink dress with a thick belt around her waist, gold necklace and earrings, and grey heels. Her dirty blonde hair was pulled back in a low bun, with a few fluffy strands escaping. They framed her face perfectly. Laura wore a long, navy blue dress with black polka dots and elbow length sleeves. Her shoulder length dark brown and blue streaked hair looked effortless: completely untouched yet completely perfect all at once. That summed up Laura completely.

"Thank you, Lynne," Laura grinned as she hugged her.

"How are things going here?" Cassidy asked hugging her mother next.

"Oh, my goodness," Lynne let out a dramatic sigh.

"Here, come over here," Cassidy said, leading her mom away from the coat wall and to the far side of the narthex, Laura in step.

"What's going on?" Laura asked.

"Honestly, I'm so happy I'm the mother of the groom. It's just so much -- and I've got it easy compared to Ellie's mom," Lynne said. Laura snorted while Cassidy shook her head.

"Is everything going smoothly?" Laura asked.

"As far as I can tell, yes," Lynne nodded.

"Anyone drunk yet?" Cassidy asked playfully with a raised eyebrow.

"Benjamin may be a little tipsy," Lynne rolled her eyes.

"Excellent," Cassidy smirked.

"Anything you need?" Laura asked.

"No, no, honestly, I don't have much to do other than wait for Alex's cue for Dad to walk me down the aisle to our seats."

"That's good," Cassidy smiled.

"No, it's not! I'm all hyped up and anxious for no reason."

"Your son is getting married; you're supposed to be excited," Cassidy told her.

"Very excited!" Laura added. Lynne gave a small sigh.

"I guess guests will be arriving soon."

"You can help greet," Cassidy said.

"Yes! Remember, Cassidy and I showed up forty-five minutes early because we're family. Most people won't get here until less than thirty minutes to the start," Laura added.

"Are we the first people here other than the bridal party and such?" Cassidy asked, glancing around.

"Nonna and Pap arrived an hour early, as per usual," Lynne grumbled, referencing Art's parents who had a propensity for showing up at events significantly earlier than expected or wanted.

"Nonna and Pap are here? Where?" Cassidy asked excitedly. She loved her grandparents, quirks and all.

"Yes, yes, they insisted on holding their seats." Lynne gestured toward the sanctuary. "Art is with them. I told him that he can't let Pap start talking about Jimmy The Greek to everyone that sits near them." Laura gave a snort.

"I'll go in and steer the conversation to Willie Mays," Cassidy grinned.

"That's baseball; he can easily shift the conversation," Lynne warned.

"Lynne, we've got a few minutes, want to go out and have a quick cig with me?" Laura offered, pulling the half open pack out of her purse.

"Eh, what the hell," Lynne shrugged.

"Mom!"

"Go see your grandparents, and make sure your dad hasn't taken off his shoes," Lynne instructed before hastily following Laura outside. Cassidy shook her head before turning and heading into the mostly empty sanctuary.

It was about five minutes to three and the sanctuary had filled up considerably. Cassidy and Laura were seated in the second row from the front, Nonna and Pap right behind them. Cassidy attempted to be a sound shield between Pap's commentary and her mother's ears in the front row. The right side of the church was filled with cousins, old neighbors, former classmates, and friends of Eric and the whole Banker family. There was the slightly odd paradox of Cassidy seeing people she had gone to school with from kindergarten through to twelfth grade that she knew of, but didn't know personally anymore. They had been in different social circles. And yet, here they were to celebrate her twin. There had been a few awkward waves. She really wasn't looking forward to the uncomfortable small talk later that evening.

The left side of the church was just as full with Ellie's family and friends. Cassidy and Laura played a little game of trying to guess who was who: cousins? aunts? friends? Their game of making up fake back-stories for the guests was interrupted by the sound of someone clearing their throat in the aisle next to her.

"Can I join you?"

Cassidy looked up and gasped. Jake was standing at the edge of the pew in a black suit and dark green tie. She immediately leapt up and hugged him.

"Oh my gosh! What are you doing here?"

"Your brothers invited me," he grinned as they pulled apart.

"Jake!" Laura beamed from her seat.

"Hey," he waved.

"Come sit," Laura said, scooting over slightly and patting the pew next to her. Jake squeezed past Cassidy and took a seat between the girls as Cassidy returned to hers.

"When did they invite you? It better not have been this morning. They are so rude!" Cassidy rolled her eyes.

"No, no," Jake chuckled. "It was after I came to dinner the other month. I got a call the next day."

"What? Why didn't you tell me?" Cassidy asked in shock, slapping his thigh playfully.

"Eric thought it would be more fun as a surprise."

Cassidy made a face, then leaned over to ask Laura, "Did you know about this?"

"No. But while Alex is many things, a scheduling savant, he is not," Laura said.

"Well, I'm glad you're here," Cassidy smiled.

"Glad to be here!"

The organ started to play a few chords and anyone who wasn't seated yet hustled to find a spot. The interlude music sounded like a familiar hymn that Cassidy simply couldn't place. The peaceful melody flowed through the sanctuary as Cassidy looked around. It was beautifully decorated in white linens with white and red flowers covering almost the entire altar. Tall red candles were lit atop the posts on either side of the pews, and a long white carpet lined the aisle.

Suddenly the melody changed and the minister appeared at the altar in white robes and a red stoll. Cassidy wondered if his color coordination with the decorations was intentional or a happy accident. Either way, it was nice. She saw him nod toward the back of the church and Cassidy turned to see her parents walking down the aisle arm in arm. Lynne was beaming. Art looked like he was trying to see who all was there; his focus was anywhere but the aisle. Cassidy grinned at them as they took their seats directly in front of her.

Next down the aisle was May Hammond, Ellie's mom. She

was being escorted by Alex. May looked quite overwhelmed, yet stunning in a deep purple dress that shimmered as she walked. Once she had been seated in the front pew opposite Art and Lynne, Alex joined Eric and the other groomsmen up front. Matty was first in line as the best man. Eric and Matty had always been the closest. Alex took his spot after Matty, with Ben just behind. Next was Derek Emig -- he and Eric had been roommates since freshman year at Pitt -- and then Jeremy Deal. Jeremy had grown up in the Banker's neighborhood and he and Eric had been friends since preschool. Cassidy smiled at her old neighbor. She hadn't seen him in years. He had gone to college down south and stayed there.

All six of them were in grey suits with red ties. Eric had a red rose and sprig of baby's breath in his front pocket. They all looked great, even Ben, who was a tad bouncy. He had definitely taken a shot or two. Cassidy watched her twin. He looked happy. He smiled at Lynne, who Cassidy could hear sniffling from the row in front of her, before he caught her eye. They shared a knowing look and a smile. This was going to be a great day!

The music changed once more and the crowd began to coo. Cassidy turned to see two young girls and a little boy, all dressed up in reds and whites, make their way down the aisle. The ring bearer and one of the flower girls were the children of Cassidy's eldest cousin. Jenny was six and Tony was four. The other flower girl was a young cousin of Ellie named Sasha. Ellie had previously mentioned that she was four, as well. Their procession went as expected. Jenny diligently tossed her flower petals while bossing the other two around to get them down the aisle. There was a brief pause as Sasha tried to pick up all the petals and put them in her basket. Jenny frantically and loudly whispered corrections to her before Sasha turned her basket over and dumped all the petals into a pile on the floor. She grinned proudly as all the guests started to laugh. Jenny shook her head in annoyance before continuing the journey on her own, proudly tossing her petals correctly and taking her seat in the front pew. Sasha then sprinted up front and was intercepted by a relative in the second row on Ellie's side. After some coaxing from the groomsmen, Tony completed his trek down the aisle, handed the pillow to Matty and ungracefully climbed up onto the pew between Art and Jenny. He grinned over the back of the pew at Cassidy who reached forward and offered him her hand in a high five which he loudly smacked before turning and sitting down.

The bridesmaids started their procession down the aisle. Mindy, Elaine, Lisa, Molly, and then Kara, all in long, scarlet red dresses with fitted bodices, A-line skirts, and poofy sleeves. As bridesmaid dresses go, they weren't bad at all. However, Cassidy was still happy she didn't have to wear one. The five bridesmaids each carried a small bouquet of white lilies and greens and all wore their hair in low buns tied with red ribbons. They all looked very pretty as they happily took their places.

The music changed a final time, the familiar wedding march began, and everyone rose to their feet. Ellie and her father appeared at the end of the aisle. Ellie looked gorgeous. Her long, black hair was in an elaborate up-do. Her diamond white wedding dress was beyond stunning. The skirt was somewhere between A-line and ballgown with lace designs along the hem. The bodice had a low neck-line and the fabric ruched to the left side of her body; a large white bow sat on her left hip. Short, puffy sleeves rested on her shoulders, but otherwise her arms were bare aside from her white satin gloves.

Cassidy gasped at the sight of her, but quickly looked back to catch the face on her brother, who looked like he was about to fall over. She giggled slightly before turning her attention back to the bride.

The service went smoothly. The mothers in the front pews both sniffled through the entire thing, and Jeremy stifled multiple sneezes; he was standing next to one of the large floral stands and was quite evidently allergic.

The church erupted in cheers at the kiss, and the music played loudly and joyfully as the couple exited hand in hand, followed by Matty and Kara, Alex and Molly, Ben and Lisa, Derek and Elaine, and Jeremy and Mindy.

The reception was held in the ballroom of a large hotel. The red and white theme continued with tablecloths, flowers, and candles all about the cavernous room.

While everyone was milling around during the cocktail hour, Cassidy was pulled out of the room by the photographer to get some family pictures with her parents, brothers and Ellie. When the photo shoot finally ended, Cassidy greeted Eric with a hug.

"Congratulations!"

"Thank you!"

"Everything went very well," she smiled as she pulled back.

"Yeah, it was weird."

"A Banker family event that ran smoothly. We need to document this!"

"I'm thrilled the ceremony went well, but I'm sure we'll find a way to make a scene here," Eric chuckled.

"Oh, come on. We've got this."

"Have you seen Ben?" Eric asked, nodding slightly behind him. Cassidy peered around his shoulder and saw Ben clip a chair with his hip and stumble slightly. He did look unsteady.

"Mom said he was tipsy before the ceremony. At this rate, he'll be shitfaced by the end of the night. He didn't drive, did he?"

"No, Mom and Dad picked him up and brought him. I don't think they trusted him getting here on time."

"Smart, but where did he get the booze?"

"Remember Matty gave him that flask for his last birthday?"

"Oh jeez," Cassidy rolled her eyes.

"There's an open bar. Everyone else will catch up to him soon, so it'll be fine."

"True." She shrugged before she was blindsided with a tackling hug from her left. Cassidy toddled to steady herself a bit.

"Sister!" Ellie squealed.

"Heyyy!! Congratulations!" Cassidy hugged her back.

"Thank you!" Ellie slowly loosened her bear hug and moved to stand next to Eric, still bouncing on her heels slightly. Cassidy loved seeing her so happy. It was contagious.

"Everything was beautiful – and you look gorgeous!" Cassidy gushed.

"Thank you! It feels like a dream," she grinned. Eric kissed her on the cheek.

"Yinz deserve it," Cassidy said honestly. She could see how happy they were -- and she was happy for them. It wasn't just avoiding the drama and stress of being in the bridal party, or the ceremony being disaster free, or even her enjoyment of watching Ben being scolded quietly like a child by Lynne after accidentally backing into a planter and knocking dirt on the carpet, but Cassidy felt real joy.

"Jake looked quite handsome," Ellie smirked.

"Yes, and, thank you guys for inviting him! I don't know why you made it all secretive, but it was a nice surprise," Cassidy said.

"We like him," Eric smiled with a small shrug.

"I do, too."

Cassidy and Jake found themselves seated at a table with Art and Lynne, Laura, Nonna and Pap, and Lynne's brother, Leo, who had never married and was currently in between girlfriends. They were seated less than twenty feet from the head table where the entire bridal party sat, which Cassidy would have enjoyed significantly more if the bridesmaid seated closest to her wasn't complaining constantly. Ellie's older sister, Kara, had a comment about everything, from decor, to food, to music, politics, fashion, and anything else she could think of. This was the fourth time Cassidy had met Kara and she enjoyed her as much as she had enjoyed working with Devon Parks.

Cassidy did her best to focus on her table. She was seated between Jake and Laura, as Art had insisted Jake sit next to him to talk with him all about sports statistics. The dinner was delicious. Cassidy, Lynne, Pap, and Uncle Leo all enjoyed the lemon parmesan chicken with rice and green beans, while Jake, Art, Laura, and Nonna selected the roast beef, smashed potatoes, and green beans choice. Everyone was thrilled and stuffed to the gills.

Matty gave a best man speech in which he managed to weave in the story of Eric spilling his blue slushie all over his date at the movies when he was in ninth grade. Cassidy had actually forgotten about that one! But after a solid laugh from the crowd, and an eye roll from Eric, Matty teased that his dating skills had obviously improved to be able to even get a first date with Ellie. The speech was sweet and everyone smiled and clapped at the end as Matty hugged the newlyweds before taking his seat once more.

Kara was up next. After a failed attempt at a shoe joke, she told a story about herself, before saying the wedding was beautiful and raising a toast. Everyone grimaced slightly as they clapped. Ellie and Eric were good sports about the whole thing, but they looked thrilled for the dancing to begin.

After the traditional first dances, the DJ turned up "Crocodile Rock" and everyone hit the dance floor. Thank you, Elton!

The Bankers and the Narleskis, Lynne's side of the family, all loved a good dance party and weren't afraid to let loose. They were very happy to find that the Hammond family joined the party without hesitation.

Jake allowed himself to be pulled along by Cassidy, and while his efforts were in full force, Cassidy -- and everyone in a five-foot radius -- were quickly made aware that he was not a great dancer. That didn't stop him though, and Cassidy appreciated that. The safety and bone structure of her toes aside, she didn't want someone who sat on the sidelines. She loved that he was out there dancing just as hard as she was, and having a great time!

After four songs, a break to hit the open bar, and another two songs, the DJ slowed it down with a Platters song. Over half the dance floor emptied, but about twenty couples stayed,

Cassidy and Jake included. He wrapped his arms around her waist and she rested her forearms on his shoulders.

"Thank God," Jake sighed.

"You missed holding me?"

"No, I was tired," he replied. Cassidy gasped in mock outrage before laughing.

"Spaz."

"I missed you, too," he smirked, placing a light peck on her lips.

"I'm so glad you're here today."

"I am, too."

"Are you having fun?" she asked as they swayed with the music.

"A lot of fun! Your family is…"

"There are a lot of adjectives you could put in there."

"Fun."

"Fun?"

"Yes. I mean it's loud and chaotic and everyone fights, but you all love each other and just make everything more fun than it would be with my family," Jake said.

"Thank you?" Cassidy giggled.

"It's a compliment."

"I like that they don't scare you off."

"Oh, they scare the hell out of me," Jake said.

"But we're fun!"

"Exactly."

Cassidy hugged him tightly to her as they continued to sway with the music. She smiled into his shoulder.

"You know, I can't remember the last time I slow danced," Jake said in a low voice next to her ear.

"Yeah?"

"I think it was high school. What about you?"

"Um, my cousin Ericka's wedding, like, two years ago," Cassidy told him.

"What song?" he asked.

"Oh, I have no idea," Cassidy chuckled.

"Really?"

"Off the top of my head, no. What song was yours?"

"We've Got Tonight."

"Bob Segar? Oh, that's a good one."

"Yes."

"Why do you still remember it?"

"Senior prom."

"Ah, you went with Molly?" Cassidy asked, pulling back to look up at him. They had talked about previous relationships. Molly was his best friend who had become his first girlfriend the last two years of high school. They parted on good terms when they both left for different colleges, and were still friends to this day.

"Yeah, we had a blast. One of our last weekends as a couple, just having fun. Because after that it was finals and graduation. We both worked in the summer and then we left for college."

"Do you miss hanging out with her all the time?" Cassidy asked. Jake shook his head.

"A bit. But not in a romantic way. She was always my friend more than anything. I was just trying to remember the last time I danced like this."

"That makes sense," she smiled. Jake leaned down and placed a sweet kiss on her lips as the final note crooned out over the speakers. They pulled back and grinned at each other.

"Wanna take a break?" Jake asked as "Walk Like an Egyptian" started up. Cassidy nodded and took his hand. They weaved their way off the dance floor and out of the reception hall into the hallway.

"Wow, it's like, twenty degrees cooler out here!" Cassidy said, fanning herself.

"A lot less people."

"This place is gorgeous!" Cassidy said, slowly spinning as she took in the large corridor. "Laura and I came in with the herd; I didn't really take it all in."

"Want to take a few minutes to explore?" Jake asked, holding out his hand.

"Sure," Cassidy grinned and linked her hand in his. They walked down the beautifully decorated corridor into the spacious lobby filled with high end sofas, art, a massive glass chandelier, and a piano with a pianist, most likely hired to attempt to drown out the noise of the reception. They admired the space before continuing along toward the opposite side of the hotel with another corridor that mirrored theirs. There were a few smaller event rooms on this side. As Cassidy and Jake passed Conference Room C they heard the sound of chairs crashing. They paused and looked at each other for a moment before Jake reached out and cautiously pushed the door open. Cassidy gaped in shock when she suddenly found herself in full view of her younger brother making out with a bridesmaid. Jake gave a low chuckle. Ben and Lisa, Ellie's college roommate, were stumbling as they frantically and passionately kissed. Ben's jacket was on the floor and his white dress shirt was untucked and unbuttoned; Lisa's red bridesmaid dress was off her shoulders bunched at her waist. Her dark curly hair was frizzing out of her formerly neat bun. It took about two seconds for them to realize they had been interrupted.

"Ugh! Cassidy! Get out!" Ben said angrily.

"Shit!" Lisa said, pulling back from Ben and crossing her arms over her chest.

"Sorry, man." Jake gave a low laugh and tugged Cassidy away.

"Get lost, Cassidy!" Ben yelled. Cassidy couldn't think of a good comeback and just laughed before following Jake out of the room and closing the door behind them.

"Oh no!" she said breathily, still in shock.

"Well, he's having a good time," Jake smirked as they slowly walked away from the room.

"Seriously! Come on, let's get back to the reception," Cassidy said, taking his hand and pulling him along.

"Ready to dance more?"

"Yes, but also I have to tell Laura!" she said. Jake laughed, following her back to the large banquet hall on the other side of the hotel.

The last hour of the reception was more fun. There was lots of dancing, and lots of drinks. When Jake took breaks to talk with Art about baseball, Cassidy danced with Matty, who introduced her to a bunch of Ellie's cousins he had hit it off with –he could make friends every single place he went. He was fun!

Ben and Lisa reappeared with less than fifteen minutes left in the night. Lisa had cut her losses and pulled her curly hair up into a ponytail rather than trying to repair the neat bun. Cassidy and Laura giggled childishly as Ben walked by and he shot them an annoyed glare, which made them laugh even harder.

The final song of the night was "Shout" by the Isley Brothers. Every single person was on the dance floor. Cassidy's favorite part of the night was watching everyone do the little bit softer now part before easing back up to standing and jumping.

Once the lights were back on and the DJ was prepping everyone to see the newlyweds off, Ellie ran over to Cassidy, who was standing with Laura.

"Hi!" she grinned.

"Hi!" Cassidy said.

"Everything was perfect! Did you think it was perfect?" Laura asked.

"Yes, definitely."

"Is Kara okay? I've hardly seen her since dinner," Cassidy wondered as she spotted the maid of honor standing apart from everyone and looking annoyed. Ellie grimaced.

"Oh, I feel bad. She apparently really likes Derek, but he didn't even want to dance with her. She's taking it pretty hard. I think she thought they'd start dating tonight."

"Poor girl," Cassidy said.

"Not everyone struck out." Laura smirked and wiggled her eyebrows, making Cassidy laugh.

"What?" Ellie asked.

Laura leaned in and whispered. "Ben and Lisa."

"What?" Ellie gasped. Both Cassidy and Laura nodded.

"Yep."

"Can we have Eric and Ellie over here, please?" The DJ called over the mic.

"Oh, I've got to go, but I want to hear more!"

"You have a great time! We'll get together for drinks when you get back from the honeymoon!" Laura said.

"Really?"

"Absolutely, can't wait!" Cassidy said, giving her hand a squeeze before Ellie happily ran over to Eric.

Eric and Ellie were staying in the honeymoon suite at the hotel for the night so rice was tossed at them in the reception room as they ran through the parted crowd, laughing the whole way, before they were led to the private elevator by one of the staff members.

After lots of hugs and goodbyes with family and friends, and Cassidy gently asking Lynne to stop crying for the fifth time since the rice throwing, Cassidy was bundled up in her winter coat once more and walking with Jake through the dark, cold parking lot to his car.

"This was a fantastic day," she said as they reached his car.

"Yeah, it was. It was pretty perfect."

"But that's the thing! It wasn't perfect -- not at all -- but it was fantastic! And I'm so happy right now."

"I'm happy you're so happy," Jake said, leaning down and kissing her.

Chapter 17

Cassidy stirred her peach margarita with her straw as she sat at the small, round table with Laura and Ellie. It was two weeks after Eric and Ellie's wedding, and they had only returned home from their honeymoon a few days prior. As the girls had promised at the reception, they met up for drinks -- and Cassidy was having a wonderful time. The three women had been at the restaurant for the last hour and a half, and all of them were just starting their third drink.

"Come on, what was your favorite part of Jamaica?" Laura asked, taking a sip of her wine.

"The heat!" Ellie replied with a smile. It was February in Erie. It hadn't been above freezing all week and there were five inches of snow on the ground. That Caribbean sun must have been fantastic, Cassidy thought.

"Oh, I can only imagine," Cassidy smiled.

"The heat outside or the heat in the hotel room?" Laura asked with a wink. Ellie giggled and blushed. Cassidy scrunched up her nose.

"Ellie, I'm happy you're happy, but please do not go into detail while I'm here. Please!" Cassidy begged. Laura cackled.

"Ignore her, she's scared of sex," Laura said to Ellie. Cassidy shook her head in shock.

"What the hell are you talking about?"

"Come on, you never let me talk about my sex life," Laura pointed out.

"Oh my god, you two are fucking my brothers!" Cassidy enunciated. Laura and Ellie shared a look before laughing hysterically.

"If we weren't fucking your brothers, you wouldn't get to hang out with us here tonight!" Laura pointed out. Cassidy smiled and nodded.

"Very true," she admitted. Laura laughed.

"But Eric and I did have a good time," Ellie grinned. Laura nodded and grinned back while Cassidy took a large gulp of her margarita, choosing to ignore them. She honestly was happy they were happy, and that her brothers were. She just didn't want to hear any bedroom details.

"Alright, to appease Cassidy, let's change this up slightly," Laura began.

Cassidy perked up.

"Who was your first? And was it good or bad?" Laura asked.

"Oh, boy," Ellie sighed. "I need a shot for that."

Cassidy let out a snort.

"Deal!" Laura agreed. She quickly flagged down the server and ordered three shots of rum, which were brought out a few minutes later, the three of them laughing hysterically. Clearly their earlier drinks were starting to hit. Cassidy was thrilled she didn't have to drive that night. Eric, Alex, and Jake were hanging out at the loft and had promised to pick them up after the hockey game ended on TV.

"Alright, shoot on three?" Cassidy asked, now that they each had a full shot glass in their hands.

The girls nodded, tapped their glasses three times on the table and tossed them back. All three gasped as the liquor hit.

"Yikes," Ellie laughed.

"Yeah," Cassidy agreed.

"Okay, okay," Laura said, her voice was starting to slur, which made Cassidy laugh. She was drunk.

"Okay," Cassidy teased.

"We got our shots, now we all have to tell… How good -- or bad -- was your first time?" Laura asked.

"I think weird is a better word," Ellie said with a giggle.

"Alright, Ellie, you're up first, spill," Laura pushed.

"How old were you?" Cassidy asked as she took another sip of her margarita. Her head was starting to buzz. The last time she'd been this tipsy she'd been at the club with Marissa and ended up going home with Pete. That felt like a lifetime ago, but really it had been less than a year. Damn.

"I was eighteen," Ellie began, shifting in her seat. Cassidy could see a blush coming on. "It was freshman year at Penn State. There was a huge Halloween party in my dorm. My roommate and I came dressed as the Pink Ladies from Grease. It was a great party. There was a guy from the floor above me. I saw him practically every day, he always said hi. Well, wouldn't you know it, he showed up as Danny Zucko. We spotted each other immediately and spent the whole party talking and laughing, and drinking a lot. Then he brought me up to his dorm room. His roommate was out all night so we had the room to ourselves. He kissed me the second he shut

173

the door. I remember it all moving pretty quickly. I remember being super hot, probably from all the alcohol. Our clothes came off so fast. He was on top of me, we were both sweaty because those dorms didn't have A/C, and even though it was late October, there were so many students there that night. It was hot as hell." Ellie sighed before taking another drink from her glass.

"And how was it?" Cassidy asked, intrigued.

"Well, I just remember that I was shocked there was no, like, warning! Just, mmmmm! He was in!" Ellie said with an accompanying hand gesture. Both Laura and Cassidy snorted in laughter.

"Mmmmm, huh?" Laura asked, still chuckling.

"I guess so. It hurt more than I was ready for and I had no idea what to expect, honestly," Ellie laughed.

"Oooof," Cassidy sighed.

"But then it was done, we kissed, and he rolled off of me, and I felt suddenly super aware that I was naked in some dude's room…" Ellie trailed off.

"Did you guys ever do it again?" Cassidy asked. Ellie shook her head.

"Nope, we just laid there for like five minutes. I sat up and got dressed, he did, too. We made out for a bit and then left and went back to the party," Ellie shrugged.

"Hmmm," Laura mumbled, clearly in thought.

"I'm not mad at him. We never dated, or had any other… encounters, but we smiled and waved at each other every time we saw each other in the halls for the rest of the year. We were both in different dorms our sophomore year, and honestly, I don't even know what happened to him."

"I think that's a pretty good first time," Cassidy said.

"Honestly, it wasn't bad. He was nice, and he was cute," Ellie said with a smile.

"I think it's pretty good one," Laura said before taking a sip.

"Okay, then you're up next," Cassidy nodded pointedly at Laura.

"Oh boy," Laura began with a large grin.

"Come on, you have to tell us!" Ellie pushed, smiling back.

"I don't know if Cassidy will like it," Laura shrugged. Cassidy felt her face scrunch up in confusion.

"Why?" Cassidy asked.

"Because my first time was actually with Alex," Laura shrugged, the grin not leaving her face. Cassidy's eyebrows shot up in surprise.

"Really?" Both Cassidy and Ellie asked in unison.

"Yes, really!" Laura responded defensively. Cassidy shook her head.

"No, I -- I was just surprised…" she trailed off.

"Why?" Laura asked.

"I don't know!"

"Well, tell us about it!" Ellie pushed, smacking her palm on the table.

"Just not all the details," Cassidy added.

"No, all the details!" Ellie interjected. Laura gave a hard laugh and Cassidy took another large gulp to prepare.

"Okay, okay." Laura took a sip of her drink then launched into her story.

"Alex and I met the first day of class our sophomore year at MU. We had a creative writing class together. We just happened to sit next to each other on the first day and stayed there the whole semester. We didn't have our first date for a few weeks; we went out to one of the clubs downtown. But it was after our third date – we went to the movies -- that he invited me back to his dorm. His roommate had gone home for the weekend."

"That third date rule," Cassidy chuckled sarcastically.

"Yes, well, I knew something was going to happen that night, but I wasn't sure what. We had only shared a few kisses. Actually, our longest make-out session had been at the movies earlier that night. I've still never seen Death on the Nile in full," Laura admitted.

Both Cassidy and Ellie laughed and shared a smirk.

"He turned on the record player as soon as we got in the room… I looked around at all his books and posters, and suddenly he was standing right behind me. I turned around to face him and we kissed. It was pure adrenaline. But he was so sweet with me. We took our time. He just kissed me so good that night. I felt really hot and excited. I remember being oddly comfortable with him as my clothes came off. And then the moment came, we were in bed, and I knew it was going to happen. That's when my nerves kicked in, but he just cuddled me and calmed me right down. It honestly was a great night."

"Oh my God, that is so freaking sweet," Ellie gushed. "Those Banker boys."

Laura giggled, and Cassidy forced herself to not roll her eyes. She loved her brothers, but hearing about them in romantic moments was not her favorite thing.

"I, I'm, uh, glad it was so good." Cassidy took another sip.

"I'm sorry, Cassidy, I know it wasn't what you wanted to hear," Laura chuckled.

"It's what I wanted to hear!" Ellie pipped in, causing Laura to giggle.

"I'm glad you enjoyed my story, at least," Laura said.

"No, no, I'm happy. It's just, it's my brother..." Cassidy shuddered.

"I get it," Laura admitted.

"Anything else happen that night?" Ellie asked curiously.

"No, not really. I mean afterwards, we stayed in bed for like thirty minutes. Like we just rested together and shared a cigarette," Laura said.

"Awww," Cassidy said halfheartedly.

"I think it helped that he knew what he was doing, and just his general demeanor made it great for me. I remember immediately thinking that I wanted to be with him forever. And we've been together since," Laura gushed.

"Oh my gosh, I love that!" Ellie grinned. Cassidy nodded.

"Shot? Anyone?" Cassidy asked with a slight slur.

"You're shitfaced already," Laura commented with a chuckle.

"I'm drunk, but definitely not shitfaced," Cassidy countered with a hiccup, causing all three of them to burst into another fit of laughter.

"Well, before you pass out, we need your story," Ellie enunciated. Cassidy laughed and bit her lip. Her first time was not a story she readily shared. As a matter of fact, Marissa was the only person she'd ever told.

"Come on! We told you ours," Laura pointed out. Cassidy sighed.

"I've only ever told one person about it before," Cassidy blushed.

"A secret?" Ellie asked excitedly, leaning in.

"You have to tell us now! No backing out!" Laura said. Cassidy started to nervously laugh.

"What?" Ellie asked in a laugh, enjoying the moment.

"I fucked Alex's friend," Cassidy laughed, waving her hands in a shrug.

"Wait, what?" Ellie asked, her eyes wide as she laughed along.

"Which one?" Laura asked frantically.

"Tommy," Cassidy admitted, resting her hand on her forehead in playful shame.

"Oh, I remember him. They were friends all through high school and college, then Tommy moved out to Colorado, and we haven't seen him in years," Laura said. Cassidy nodded. She was well aware.

"Was he cute?" Ellie asked Laura.

"Very," Laura nodded. "I need to hear this story! I can't believe I haven't heard it before," Laura said excitedly.

"Honestly, it's so dumb. Tommy stopped by one afternoon in summer. Alex was still at work -- he worked at the pizza shop on North Street back then. But Tommy stayed at the house to hang out and wait for him. I'm not sure how it happened, but we ended up hanging out, just him and me. We were just talking and telling stories, then out of nowhere, he kissed me. Oh, man, I was so excited. I had such a crush on him. Suddenly, we were making out. Then he pushed me back on the bed and his hands were up my shirt. I thought I was so cool. Before I knew it, he had my shorts off, and his were, too. It didn't last long, but holy shit," Cassidy said.

"Good shit or bad?" Laura chuckled.

"I thought good. Dude, I had a million thoughts racing through my head that afternoon. I remember being excited and scared and just freaking out. I had no idea what I was supposed to be doing," Cassidy explained. "But it was done, and before I knew it and he was climbing off of me. I was very aware my shorts were on the floor and my top was pushed over my boobs. Tommy was already getting dressed, so I did, too. He pulled me in for a hug and we made out for a few more minutes. Then he said that he had to go."

"That's shitty," Ellie scrunched up her face.

"It's not shitty. I mean, honestly, the timing was good. As he was going down the stairs, Alex came in the front door from work, so we weren't caught. But we never did it again. I was always kind of hoping that we would. I stupidly thought it meant we were going to date. We never did. We went back to just him being friends with my brother and saying hi to me occasionally." Cassidy shrugged.

"Ugh," Laura sighed.

"Don't look at me like that! It's fine!" Cassidy said, looking at their pitying faces. "This is why I never tell this dumbass story. Honestly, it was good that it happened. I was home, I was safe, and I learned that real-life fairytale romance isn't real. It was good to get my bubble burst."

"How old were you?" Ellie asked.

"Sixteen," Cassidy said. "I was old enough to learn. I mean, I thought I had a chance with him. I was an idiot!"

"Only a bit of an idiot," Laura teased. All three girls burst out laughing.

"I'm glad yinz all find my dumbass teenage self as ridiculous as I do," Cassidy giggled.

"It's only funny because things are good now. Like, Jake is your fairy-tale boyfriend. So it all worked out!" Ellie said.

"Yeah, he's good. You just had to... kiss a couple of frogs first," Laura smirked.

"A lot of frogs," Cassidy sighed, rolling her eyes.

"Yeah, I remember Eric told me you were kinda slutty," Ellie commented with a hiccup. Both Cassidy and Laura gasped in shock before starting to laugh once more.

"I'm going to kill him!" Cassidy said. "That's what he says about me?"

"I think just to me, and it was a long time ago," Ellie defended her husband. "I never believed him, just assumed it was sibling humor."

"You should have believed him," Laura commented in a deadpan smirk. Cassidy turned to playfully glare at her. Laura leaned over and gave her a peck on the cheek. "But we still love you!"

"Yes! I'm so glad we're friends now. I was missing out!" Ellie added.

The girls laughed as they sipped the last of their drinks. Suddenly Eric appeared behind Ellie.

"Hey," Eric said, placing his hands on Ellie's shoulders and smirking at the inebriated state of his wife, twin, and sister-in-law.

"Hi," Ellie gushed up at him, turning to wrap her arms around his middle.

"Eric," Cassidy slurred.

"Hmm?" Eric raised his eyebrow. Cassidy could tell he wasn't taking her seriously.

"Ellie informed me that you told her that I was a slut! I can't believe that's how you talk about me," Cassidy grumbled. Laura burst out laughing while Ellie buried her face in Eric's jacket, clearly mortified.

"You've never proved me wrong," Eric grinned obnoxiously. Cassidy wanted to throw something at him. He was clearly relishing the fact that she was too drunk to fight him. If she were sober, he'd be toast.

"Such an ass," Cassidy grumbled.

"Poor baby," Eric replied half-heartedly.

"Where's Alex?" Laura asked as she finally stopped laughing.

"He's in his car out front," Eric said. "He's waiting for you and Jake's out there talking to him."

"Why'd you come in alone?" Cassidy asked.

"Because I lost rock, paper, scissors. Go get your coat on," Eric told her sarcastically.

"Okay, let's go," Laura said. Cassidy hopped off the high chair and was suddenly acutely aware of how drunk she really was. She'd been sitting and drinking for hours, and now that she was on her feet, she knew she was in trouble. Fortunately, Ellie and Laura seemed to be making similar discoveries.

"Whoa," Ellie teetered with a giggle. Eric grabbed her arm to hold her steady. With an almost comical amount of difficulty, they were able to put their coats on, grab their bags, leave cash on the table for the bill, and follow Eric through the restaurant and outside. The cold air hit them like a brick and they all let out audible gasps.

"Okay, Alex is over there," Eric said, pointing to the idling car waiting about fifty feet away. Jake was leaning over the open passenger window and chatting.

"Good," Cassidy said, happy to know she didn't have to stand out in this frigid night air for long.

"Bye girls, thanks for inviting me along!" Ellie gushed, pulling her arm out of Eric's and stumbling over to give them a hug. Cassidy and Laura immediately embraced her in a group hug.

"You're welcome out with us anytime!" Laura cheered.

"Definitely," Cassidy agreed. After a long moment, they pulled apart. Eric took ahold of Ellie's arm once more to steady her; she was starting to teeter.

"Bye, Eric!" Laura screamed, much louder than she needed to. Ellie laughed hysterically.

"See ya," Cassidy grinned at her twin. He rolled his eyes at her.

"Get in the car before everyone freezes," Eric instructed as he led Ellie in the opposite direction towards her car.

"Yeah, let's go!" Cassidy said, looking over at Laura shivering next to her.

"I'm freezing and I need another cigarette!" Laura grumbled. They walked as fast as they could towards the taillights of Alex's car. Cassidy wasn't sure how she made the short journey without face-planting, but she was thrilled when they reached the car. Alex climbed out as they approached.

"Can yinz walk?" he asked, looking at the two girls with amusement.

"Yes," Cassidy sighed. Jake chuckled as he walked over to her and wrapped his left arm around her shoulder.

"Oh my god!" Laura said as she got herself inside the car.

"So cold," Cassidy shivered against Jake.

"Aw, babe," Laura cooed as Alex handed her a cigarette from his pack on the dash. Cassidy rolled her eyes.

"Ready?" Alex asked.

"Yes. Night!" Laura yelled to Cassidy and Jake before rolling up the window. Alex put the car in gear and merged onto the street.

"Looks like you had fun," Jake said as they started to walk to the parking lot.

"Please tell me you didn't park far?" Cassidy shivered. Erie

182

folk were tough in winter, but they were also smart enough to not go out if they didn't need to. This had not been one of Cassidy's smarter moments.

"Right over here," Jake said. He helped her into his truck. The engine reluctantly fired up, clearly unhappy about the cold, as well. Cassidy held her hand over the vents waiting for warm air.

"How many drinks did you have?" Jake laughed as they turned onto the street.

"Um… three? Four? There was a shot in there, too… How many drinks did you have?" she asked playfully.

"One."

"While watching hockey?"

"I know, major faux pas," Jake smirked.

"I think the faux pas is saying faux pas while talking about ice hockey," Cassidy chortled.

"Not if I was cheering for Montreal."

"Were you cheering for Montreal?"

"Absolutely not!" Jake said firmly.

"Good!" Cassidy nodded. "How was your night?"

"It was nice! Your brothers are fun."

"Yeah," Cassidy snorted. "Just the three of you at Alex's?"

"No, we went out to that sports bar by the airport and met Matty and a bunch of his friends."

"What is happening?" she asked in a low voice. Jake chuckled.

"It was a great time. Too bad the Pens lost in overtime. But we played a few rounds of darts, watched hockey, laughed a lot… Matty is a riot," he said. Cassidy watched him drive for a bit, just sitting with a smile on her face. She felt incredibly lucky.

Chapter 18

Jake unlocked his front door and led them inside. The house was pitch black. He reached around Cassidy and flipped the light switch on the wall and his living room illuminated.

"Are you hungry?" Jake asked.

"Not really, but I do have to pee," Cassidy chuckled before dropping her purse on the ground, ripping off her coat and sprinting upstairs to the bathroom as she heard Jake laugh.

After using the bathroom and washing her hands, Cassidy ran her hands through her fluffy blonde hair as she looked in the mirror. She was still pretty tipsy, but happily she didn't look it. Her cheeks were tinged with pink, but she blamed that on the cold outside. She smiled at her reflection before departing the bathroom. The hallway was dark, but she saw a light coming from Jake's bedroom at the end of the hall.

"Hey," Cassidy said, leaning against the door frame to his room.

"Hey," he replied. He was pulling his dark green sweatshirt over his head and tossing on the foot of the bed, leaving him in his jeans and grey tee shirt.

"Damn, you look good," she said in a happy sigh. He smirked at her.

"You're not bad yourself; come here," Jake said. Cassidy walked over to him and placed her hands on his chest, immediately balling up the fabric of his tee in her fists. Jake's hands went to her lower back and held her tightly to him. Cassidy loved it. They stared at each other for a long moment before they both leaned in and crashed their mouths together, the kiss deepening on impact. Jake's left hand slid down to cup her ass through her jeans. They kissed passionately as Cassidy brought her right hand up and plunged her fingers into his copper hair. Her left hand slid down to the hem of his tee and she quickly slipped her hand underneath the fabric onto his taut skin. She let her fingers caress his chest hair as they kissed. After a long moment of their mouths moving in sync, Jake moved his hands to the base of her sweater and pulled it over her head. Cassidy wasted no time in ripping his tee shirt off of him as he slid her cami off of her. They paused for a second and locked eyes, both breathing hard with the desire they felt. Jake cupped her face with his right hand and kissed her hard. Cassidy felt her heart give a heavy thump. She wanted more. She needed more. As he kissed her, she reached back and unhooked her bra. Jake used his left hand to help pull it off her shoulders and down her arms. They were both completely bare chested. Cassidy ungracefully stepped out of the black boots she was wearing, holding onto Jake's arms for balance as they kissed. She was finally able to kick them off and slid her hands down his chest and stomach to come and rest on his belt buckle. Jake stepped himself out of his sneakers easily before pulling back and smirking at her.

"What?" Cassidy asked, smiling up at him. He shrugged.

"Just happy."

"Well, come here, I'm getting cold without you kissing me."

"I can tell," Jake winked as he glanced down at her. Cassidy didn't need to look to know that her nipples were rock hard. Jake's house was old and drafty. The Erie winters were rough.

"Maybe we should get warm in bed?"

"Maybe?" Jake said placing a kiss on her lips. Cassidy turned around to the bed behind her and pulled the blankets and top sheet down. She pivoted back around to face Jake. He immediately put his hands on her hips and gave her a playful shove backwards. She landed in a seated position on the bed. Cassidy laughed and rolled her eyes, knowing full well that Jake was watching her breasts.

"Come here," she motioned with her index finger. Jake grabbed her calves and pulled. She felt a jolt run through her body as her butt slid across the mattress until she was sitting directly in front of him. Her eyes were inches from his stomach.

Cassidy reached over and unbuckled his belt before opening the button and zipper. Jake took over and removed his jeans, pulling off his socks as he stepped out of his pants. Cassidy's eyes were drawn to the large, firm protrusion at the front of his light blue boxers. She immediately brought her hands to her waist and undid her jeans. They were barely down her hips when Jake grabbed the denim and ripped them off of her legs, leaving her in just her red panties.

"Come on," Cassidy nodded her head as she scooted back on the mattress and slid under the covers. Jake quickly slipped off his boxers and climbed into bed naked. They both reached

186

for each other and pulled close. Cassidy loved the feeling of all of his skin on hers. Their lips found each other. Her left arm wrapped around his shoulders while her right hand held onto his cheek, her thumb rubbing back and forth over his five-o-clock shadow. Jake slid his right hand down her back before slipping into her panties and firmly grabbing her bare ass. Cassidy gasped into his mouth. They continued to kiss as she moved her hands down to her waist to help him remove her final covering. Once off of her ankles, Jake wadded up the red fabric and tossed them off the bed.

Cassidy stroked her hand up and down his chest and stomach a few times before taking hold of his very firm dick. He nipped lightly at her lower lip before kissing his way down her jawline to the sensitive skin on her neck.

She moved her hand slowly at first, tracing her fingertips along his length, teasing him. A few times she felt Jake buck slightly and it made her oddly proud. Cassidy tightened her hold and began to move her hand faster.

Jake brought his lips back up to hers and kissed her four times before roughly rolling them over so he was on top. He reached down and grabbed both of her wrists and pinned them above her head.

Cassidy bit her lip excitedly as she looked up at him. He smiled before leaning down and kissing her again. Slow, deliberate kisses. Again and again. He was driving her wild. The cool air from his room was nothing to combat the heat now coming from his bed.

After a few minutes, Jake released her arms. Cassidy brought them up to his shoulders. He kissed her chin before leaning over to his left and reaching for the bedside table. Cassidy could hear him rummage in the drawer, but honestly, her focus was on his tongue trailing down her throat. She gripped his shoulders tightly and let out a gasp. Her heart was pounding; she loved every feeling that was shooting through her.

Jake finished rummaging and pulled his mouth off of her throat as he hovered over her with a square, silver packet in his hand. Cassidy took the condom out of his hands and tore the wrapper open with her teeth. She tossed aside the plastic and brought her right hand under the covers. Jake helped guide her fingers as she applied the condom to his hard dick. She slowly trailed her hand back up his chest as he pressed his lips against hers in a ravenous kiss. Cassidy smiled against his mouth as she felt his knee push her legs apart. She happily complied and rested her inner thighs on his hips. Jake positioned himself at her entrance. Cassidy gripped his shoulder when he entered her. She gasped into his mouth at the contact. Jake pulled out slightly before pushing in to the hilt. He kissed her cheek as he began to move. He started slow, almost teasing her. Cassidy felt her breathing start to pick up. Her thighs squeezed against his hips. Gradually, Jake picked up the pace. Faster and faster. His breaths were heavy and loud. Cassidy felt sparks and tingling in her extremities. She was almost panting. She clawed at his back and he kissed her lips roughly. She lost track of time as he moved, her heart about to beat out of her chest. After a few more minutes of panting, thrusting, clawing, her body tingling in ecstasy, Jake kissed her hard once more. She shuddered and tipped her head back and cried out. Jake gave a final thrust and did the same.

They both went limp.

Cassidy let out a loud breath as he pulled out and rolled off of her. She turned and kissed his shoulder as he reached under the covers and removed the condom, dropping it in the waste basket off his side of the bed. They both took a moment to lie on their backs and get their breathing under control before Jake kissed her cheek and brushed a few stray strands off her face, tucking them behind her ear.

"That was good," Cassidy smirked. Jake chuckled. He placed a light peck on her lips.

"Always good."

"True."

"I love you," he said softly. Cassidy's heart gave a thump.

"I love you, too," she smiled.

Cassidy let herself back into the apartment and hung her keys on the hook. It was a little after ten in the morning on Saturday. She was just taking off her coat when she heard Marissa call out.

"Cassidy?"

"Yeah!"

"Ugh, finally!" Marissa groaned as she stepped into the hall with her hands on her hips. She looked irritated.

"What's wrong? I thought I told you I was staying at Jake's after drinks."

"Oh, you told me that," Marissa agreed. "That's not the issue."

"What's the issue?" Cassidy asked, confused. "Oh, hey, Brandon," she said, as she spotted him sitting on the couch.

"Hey." He gave a weak smile.

"The phone has been ringing off the hook all night because of your stupid brother."

"Ugh, which one?"

"Alex," Marissa huffed. She walked over and dramatically flopped down on the couch next to Brandon, her arms folded across her chest.

"I'm sorry. He's practically nocturnal and doesn't always remember most people sleep at night. I'll call him back at lunchtime."

"No! You call him back now – see how he likes it," Marissa grumbled. Cassidy winced at her friend. Marissa was generally even-tempered, easy going, and often Cassidy's voice of reason. However, when sleep deprived, she became quite stubborn and agitated. Cassidy knew she would have to make it up to her later.

"Did he say what he wanted? You should have ignored him!"

"No, it was just… Is Cassidy there? No? Dammit… Is Cassidy there? No? Dammit. Over and over. Hard to ignore."

"I answered once," Brandon chimed in. "That didn't help. He really doesn't like me."

"Ugh," Cassidy groaned. "Fine, fine, I'll call. But I don't need an audience."

"Sure," Brandon said as he stood up. "Come on, babe."

"Why?"

"Let's go lie down."

"I'm not a child, I don't need a nap," Marissa grumbled. Cassidy and Brandon shared a quick look. They seemed to both understand they couldn't make the comment they wanted to.

"I didn't say nap, I said let's go hang out in bed," Brandon said, holding his hand out for her. Marissa paused in thought for a moment before smirking and taking Brandon's waiting hand. Cassidy shook her head as she watched them head to Marissa's bedroom. Marissa stopped at the doorway and turned to look back at Cassidy.

"Make sure to tell Alex that I hate him!"

"Oh, don't worry, I will let him know."

"Okay, good! Bye!" Marissa said, shutting the door behind her.

"Good Lord." Cassidy rolled her eyes as she heard her boombox start to play The Grass Roots. She kicked off her shoes and settled on the blue chair next to the end table where they kept the phone and dialed her brothers' number.

It rang three times before answered.

"Hello?"

"Hey Laura, it's Cassidy."

"Oh, shit."

"Well, hello to you. I had a great time last night, too," Cassidy snorted.

"Sorry."

"It's okay. Where's Alex? Still sleeping? I heard he called multiple times last night. I'm appeasing Marissa by calling to wake him up this time."

"I'm sorry, Cassidy."

"What? Why?"

"I was drunk, it slipped out. I really, really didn't think it would matter!"

"What would?"

"I told Alex that you slept with Tommy," Laura admitted in a pained voice.

"Shit." Cassidy felt her heart sink. She knew he would be annoyed. Alex always wanted to be the protective big brother and care for her. However, Cassidy had always been stubborn, loud, and head strong since early childhood. She loved her eldest brother dearly but needed him significantly less than he would have liked. Cassidy always loved having him in her corner, she couldn't lie, she abused the privilege when she didn't get her way. Yet this was a moment, a private moment, that she had handled herself as a teenager. She had wanted to. She had done something grown up, she did not want to whine like a child. The interaction with Tommy was a pivotal one in her life. Both good and bad, Cassidy had learned a lot from it. The last thing she wanted to have was her brother overreacting. But now, almost ten years later, it was about to hit her like a brick. Cassidy took a deep breath.

"Yeah."

"Is he still asleep?"

"He didn't sleep much, and I can hear him putzing around in our room."

"Well, is he getting more annoyed or calming down? When would be best to talk to him?"

"I might wait… oh, hang on," Laura trailed off. Cassidy could hear noise on the other end but Laura's hand was covering the receiver and she couldn't make anything out.

"Cassidy?" Alex's voice jolted her as he took over on the call.

"Hey. You know Marissa is furious with--"

"What the hell?" he interrupted her.

"Back at you," Cassidy grumbled. This was going to be painful.

"I can't believe you were sleeping with my best friend behind my back!"

"Alex!"

"I'm pissed."

"Clearly. But I don't know why. This was ten years ago, and--"

"And my sister and friend have been lying to me for a decade!"

"Please don't be so dramatic -- that's my job," Cassidy smirked, proud of her quip.

"Stop being cute."

"Stop being mad about something that happened so long ago that frankly did not involve you in the slightest!"

"Important people in my life hiding a relationship does involve me," Alex snapped. Cassidy clenched her jaw in annoyance. Of course, he was going to blow this out of proportion. Alex hated being left in the dark. He was going to make this worse.

"I don't know what Laura said, but she must have lost something in translation because she was drunk."

"Laura wouldn't lie to me."

"I'm not saying she did, but you're talking about it like Tommy and I had a love story. We did not. He really didn't want much to do with me after."

"I... I expect more from you Cassidy."

"Yeah? Well if you're determined to be annoyed, call Tommy and bitch him out."

"Don't you worry."

"Alex, I was kidding."

"You had plenty of boyfriends! You didn't need to insert yourself in our friendships just to have all the guys."

"Our?" Cassidy questioned. She was incredibly annoyed.

"You have four brothers... I doubt I was the only one who got a friend stolen."

"Wow! Alex... what the hell?"

"Who was the guy on the phone last night?"

"That was Marissa's boyfriend. And you owe her an apology because she is my friend."

"I'll apologize when you do."

"Okay. You're pissed, I get it. I don't know why you're upset, but I'm not apologizing just to shut you up. I didn't do anything wrong. This doesn't even sound like you."

"Well, you fucked up. Just… stay away from my friends," Alex spat and hung up the phone. Cassidy sat frozen for a long moment as the dial tone hummed in her ear.

"What. The. Hell?" she said to herself before huffing off to go shower. This was not what she wanted to come home to.

Chapter 19

Cassidy spent a lot of time at the Mercyhurst University library when Jake was working. They had more resources than the community one, including newspapers from all over the country. She started combing the classifieds of the Chicago publications to help widen her job search, and see if relocating was even an option. Cassidy and Jake had been talking a lot about his upcoming move and she was quite firm that she wasn't joining him if she didn't have a job. She hated her current situation of having to rely on her parents so much. The last thing she wanted to do was shift to being a burden to Jake.

Cassidy invested in a calling card and started calling a few ads each week. Jake was making another trip to Illinois over spring break to search for a place to live and Cassidy was planning to join him for the drive out. While he apartment hunted, Cassidy hoped to line up as many interviews as she possibly could. If she didn't get a job, it definitely wouldn't be for lack of trying.

In between scouring the out of state newspapers, Cassidy was trying to improve her cooking skills. She had never been great in the kitchen, but with her sudden need to eat on a budget, she appreciated the skill more and more. Not to mention, she enjoyed making dinner for Marissa on the evenings she worked late.

Laura came over for coffee one afternoon when the school she taught at had a half day. She still felt terrible about her slip with Alex.

"I really feel awful."

"Laura, it's okay."

"You're not mad?"

"Well, I am, but you know. You didn't say anything trying to be mean."

"I really, really didn't think it would backfire this badly," Laura said earnestly.

"Is Alex still shitty?"

"Not as bad. I mean, I think he's busy with work and whatnot so it's only when I bring up your name that he starts to grumble."

"Ugh! What did you even tell him? He seems to think that Tommy and I had this long, secret relationship. I totally get how that would hurt him, but it was one afternoon -- ten years ago!" Cassidy gave a heavy sigh.

"I'm sure he'll be over it by your family dinner in a few weeks. You know him; he gets annoyed, sulks for a few weeks, then he's fine."

"Ugh, I hope. He hasn't given me that kind of shit since he first left for college and Matty helped me move his dresser into my room so I could have two."

"You stole Alex's dresser?" Laura asked with a surprised chuckle.

"Matty helped me empty it out onto his bed. I didn't throw

out his clothes."

"Oh my God."

"Alex came home for a visit in October and just absolutely lost it when he saw his dresser missing. That was a really long weekend. I mean, it was two days, but it felt like a decade." Cassidy shuddered slightly at the memory.

"I can imagine," Laura nodded. "But you two moved on from that, you can do the same now."

"Yeah, just um, do me a favor? Do not mention the dresser incident when you get home. The last thing I need is for him to be annoyed about two things from the past." Cassidy said. Laura stifled a laugh.

"My lips are sealed. I'm sober this time, too, so I can definitely make sure to keep my mouth shut."

"Thank you," Cassidy smiled.

It was spring break; however, the term "spring" was to be used loosely. From Erie to Evanston, the ground was covered in snow. Mid-March in the Midwest was cold and wintery. They still had another couple of weeks until the ground thawed out and flowers could start to grow. Jake and Cassidy were staying in the same hotel they did last time, and it was nice that the city felt slightly more familiar this trip.

Jake took them out to dinner at a Greek restaurant the hotel front desk had recommended to them on their first night.

"How many interviews do you have lined up again?" Jake asked as he pulled at a piece of lamb with his fork.

"I have two tomorrow, none on Tuesday, but one on Wednesday, and one on Thursday," Cassidy counted off on her fingers.

"We leave Saturday and I have to be back at work on Monday. What are you going to do if you get a second interview?"

"Well," Cassidy took a sip of her wine. "If one of the first ones go well, perhaps I can get it scheduled for Friday? But depending on when things are scheduled, I can call my dad and see if he'll wire some money so I can either stay out here for a few days next week and fly home, or I can drive back another time. I don't know... I'm trying not to think about these logistics because I don't want it to be an omen."

"An omen?" Jake asked.

"Yeah, like a sign of bad things."

"No, I know what an omen is, but how do you mean it now?"

"Jake, I'm serious. I want to have a job here if I'm moving. I hate sitting around at home now; it'd be worse in a new city. If the logistics of all this get too... kooky, I, ugh, I don't know what to do," Cassidy said seriously. Jake looked down.

"It will work."

"I hope so."

"Cassidy, I love you, and I'm pretty sure you love me."

"You know I do."

"Then we can figure out logistics," Jake said determinedly. Cassidy wanted to argue but she knew it was no use. Why burst his bubble before she had to? Why burst her bubble before she had to?

She decided to change the subject. "Tell me about your apartments?"

"I'm meeting with Rick, that agent. I forget what his title is, but he helps renters find places, not buyers."

"Ahh, yeah I remember you on the phone with Rick."

"Well, he has a few places lined up tomorrow and we'll talk and branch out from there depending on what I like and what's available."

"Are you excited? What would be your dream apartment?" Cassidy asked, attempting to sound as cheerful as she could for him. Jake listed off what he wanted in the place and all the things he had seen in the listing books that Rick had mailed him last week. She smiled as she listened. He was so excited. He was going to get the perfect place. He needed to. He deserved to!

Cassidy's first interview on Monday was spectacular! It was for a financial analyst position at an engineering firm in the city. She really liked the team that interviewed her. She gave them the phone number of the hotel where she was staying and her room number in case they called this week. However, her second interview was far less successful. The HR manager at a tax office had zero interest in hiring someone from out of state and was quite snippy about it. Cassidy could barely list all of her qualifications before she was ushered back out the door, leaving her feeling quite defeated.

With no interviews on Tuesday, Cassidy joined Jake in looking at a few apartments around the area. It was a very different experience from when Cassidy and Marissa found their place in Erie four years ago. They saw a four story walk up, a two bedroom basement apartment, and a ground floor unit in an old stone building that both Jake and Cassidy agreed they would never want to be in at night. Very creepy!

On Wednesday, she interviewed at an insurance company

for an auditor position. The interview went well, but it was definitely not the job Cassidy was hoping for. While the woman interviewing her was nice, the work itself sounded terrible. Cassidy returned to the hotel after the interview, ready to have a moment to herself while Jake was at Northwestern talking to his new department head. She needed a moment alone to process everything. Cassidy unlocked the hotel door and found a slip of paper on the floor when she walked in.

MESSAGE FOR CASSIDY BANKER. ROOM 407. CALL TAKEN AT FRONT DESK – 10:42AM. DAVID PHIPPS CALLED ABOUT INVERVIEW. CALL BACK # 847-555-9322.

It was hand-written on a piece of hotel stationary. Cassidy stared at it for a moment before letting out a squeal. David Phipps was one of the people who had interviewed her for the financial analyst position at the engineering firm on Monday.

She quickly shut the door behind her, shimmied off her coat and took a seat on the bed as she rummaged through her purse for her phone card.

The phone barely rang twice before it was picked up.

"Good Morning, Franklin Engineering, Rosa speaking. How may I direct your call?"

"Good Morning, Rosa. Cassidy Banker returning Mr. Phipp's call," Cassidy said as professionally as she could. In reality, her heart was pounding in her ears.

"Let me see if he's available," Rosa said before putting the call on hold. Classical music filled the line. Cassidy wondered if it was supposed to be soothing. It wasn't. She anxiously waited for just over a minute -- the equivalent of twelve minutes in hold music time -- before Rosa came back on the line.

"Ms. Banker?"

"Yes?"

"Mr. Phipps is ready to take your call. I'll transfer you."

"Thanks," Cassidy said. There were two loud clicks.

"Hello," a strong male voice answered.

"Um, hi, this is Cassidy Banker returning your--"

"Ah! Ms. Banker. You return calls quickly," Mr. Phipps remarked.

"Yes, yes, I try," Cassidy replied, frantically looking at her watch. She hadn't checked the time before calling. It was 11:13AM. Pretty good turn-around time.

"Well, I wanted to reach out and see if you're available for a second interview."

"Yes! Yes, thank you," Cassidy rambled before biting her lip. She had to sound professional, not like someone three months out of work and on her last prayer.

"Alright, can you come in tomorrow at 2PM?" Mr. Phipps asked. Cassidy dug in her purse once more for her mini date book. She had an interview with another tax agency at ten the same day.

"Yes, I can be there."

"Wonderful. You'll be meeting with the panel from Monday as well as one of our VPs."

"Looking forward to meeting them," Cassidy replied honestly.

"I've got you on the calendar; just check in with Rosa when you arrive. See you tomorrow."

"Thank you! See you tomorrow, Mr. Phipps," Cassidy said before hanging up the phone. Cassidy picked up a pillow and screamed into it. She couldn't wait to tell Jake!

Cassidy kept her Thursday morning interview. It was for a very similar job to her previous tax agency interview. While this one went very well, and Cassidy would honestly be quite happy to work there, there were thirteen other CPAs in the waiting room lined up for interviews. Talk about a confidence shaker.

Jake took her out to lunch and did not let her have the lunch special margarita that she desperately wanted. They walked around the city and found a park to relax in before he dropped her off for her second interview at Franklin Engineering.

Rosa led her to the same conference room she'd been in the first time and offered her a glass of water while she waited. Mr. Phipps and the rest of the panel – Mr. Tochet, Mrs. Reed, and Mr. Coomer -- greeted her warmly. She was introduced to the Vice President, Mr. Myers, an older man dressed in an expensive-looking grey suit, complete with a red bowtie. This man was old money if she had ever seen it.

The interview followed a similar pattern to the first. She answered all the questions confidently and made sure to ask a few of her own. Everyone seemed quite happy.

"Now, Cassidy," Mr. Myers began. "I do see that you have your address listed as Erie, Pennsylvania."

"Yes, sir. I am from there and currently live there, but I'm in the process of relocating to the Chicago area," Cassidy replied honestly.

"What brings you here? It can't be the weather," Mr. Myers joked. Cassidy gave a small, polite laugh.

"Well, I'm quite used to snow, so it won't scare me away."

"But what is the reason for this move?" Mr. Phipps asked. Cassidy bit her tongue. She refused to say that she was following a boy. That was not going to get her hired.

"I'm ready for a change. I'm twenty-six, and I've spent my whole life in Northwest Pennsylvania. While I love it and it will always be home, I... I want to step out of my bubble. Try something new," she said.

"That's admirable. Especially for a young person who isn't moving to New York or LA in hopes of becoming famous," Mrs. Reed said. Cassidy smiled at her.

"I definitely wouldn't make it in the entertainment world. I'll stick to numbers."

"Numbers are important," Mr. Phipps nodded. "Cassidy -- Ms. Banker."

"Cassidy is fine."

"Cassidy, can you excuse us for a few minutes, please?"

"Oh, um, sure... should I go out to reception, or..?"

"You can stay here. One of us will be back shortly," Mr. Phipps said. Cassidy nodded and smiled as she watched the five of them depart and close the door behind them. She let out a shaky breath. This was very stressful. Cassidy downed the remaining contents of her water glass in a single gulp. She wished she had something to distract her. The room had a few framed certificates of local awards and a large black and white photograph a man from many years ago – possibly the founder? Cassidy stood up and stretched as she walked over to the large window. The office was on the second floor and the window looked out over the street. While there was a fair amount of traffic, it was far from distracting enough to help Cassidy pass the time. She slowly made a lap around the conference room, reading all of the certificates and news articles that hung on the walls. She was just about halfway through a Chicago Tribune article from 1978 when the door opened.

"Thank you for your patience," Mr. Phipps said, closing the door behind him. Cassidy couldn't help but notice that he was alone.

"Not a problem. I enjoyed the reading," Cassidy lied with a smile as she retook her seat and he sat across from her.

"Well, I think the dry reading will have been worth it," Mr. Phipps smirked at her. "I spoke with my colleagues, and we would like to offer you a position here at Franklin Engineering."

"Oh!" Cassidy gasped. She felt the wind being knocked out of her. "Wow, thank you!"

"Yes, I've outlined the offer here for you to review." He passed over a manilla folder. Cassidy opened it. The first thing she spotted was the salary – almost double what she made in Erie. She tried to remind herself that the Chicago area was far more expensive, but still, it was an impressive number. The list of responsibilities and duties all fell within what they had discussed, and she felt confident that she could do or learn everything asked of her. Normal hours – Monday thru Friday, 9AM to 6PM with an hour for lunch. Honestly, she was excited for a full hour break in the day. Lunches at her last company were scarfing down food in the break room before running back to her desk to answer the phone. Everything looked perfect. There was one big question that stood in front of her, though.

"Mr. Phipps, this all looks great, but I do have to ask, when is the start date? As you know, I'm from Pennsylvania, and while I can start soon, unfortunately, it cannot be immediately," Cassidy said nervously, mentally praying this didn't knock the offer off the table.

"Yes, we are aware of your situation. We are willing to

work with you on this. If you are interested in accepting the offer of employment, we can delay your start, but would ask that you complete the training manual before starting and take an exam on it on your first day. That is why we offered a lower starting salary -- however, that has potential to increase after six months, depending on your performance," Mr. Phipps explained. Cassidy worked extremely hard to keep her face straight. That was the lowball salary? Damn!

"I really appreciate that. Everything sounds more than reasonable."

"I'm glad to hear."

"So, um, do I sign this paper? What do I need to do to accept?" Cassidy asked. She could hear her voice shake and took a deep breath to control it.

Mr. Phipps had her sign and date both her copy and his, and he signed and dated below her. After a few pleasantries exchanged, he asked Cassidy to return on Monday to pick up the training material, as they did not have that prepared at the moment. Cassidy assured him that she could easily do that. while deep down she knew she would be calling her father for another loan that evening.

She took the bus back toward the hotel and was left with just a five block walk. She could do it. She could figure this all out.

Raymond Phipps

Cassidy Banker

3-24-88

3-24-88

Jake hopped up from where he was lounging on the bed when she walked back into their hotel room.

"So?" He asked anxiously as she closed the door behind her and set her bag down on the dresser.

"I got it!" Cassidy squealed.

"Holy shit!" Jake ran over and scooped her up in a tight hug, lifting her off the ground and spinning twice. Cassidy laughed and cried and hugged him tightly back.

"Oh, my gosh!" she said as she set her down. Her heart was beating a mile a minute. This was the first time she let herself truly react to the news.

"Does this mean you're going to move?"

"Well, I signed the offer, so I better move or it's one hell of a commute," she chortled.

"We're… we're really moving to Illinois?" he asked. Cassidy saw tears start to form in his eyes.

"Yes! Yes, I think we are!"

"I love you so much!" Jake breathed as he pulled her into another tight hug. He gave a slight sniffle. Cassidy was touched by how happy he was. She was still in disbelief.

"I love you, too!"

"Okay," Jake said, pulling back, and clearly trying to settle himself. "Want to go look at some apartments with me?"

"Yeah. Yeah, that would probably help," she grinned.

"Great! I have another appointment with my agent in an hour."

"Perfect," Cassidy smiled. "I need to be back to call my dad before it is too late there."

"He'll be thrilled."

"Um, maybe… but I have to ask for another loan to stay a couple of extra nights and then either a plane or bus ticket home next week."

"Really?"

"Yeah, I need to go in on Monday to get my training stuff. They're willing to delay my start date, so I couldn't say I couldn't wait around a few more days."

"When do you start?"

"I have up to eight weeks," Cassidy said. It sounded both really far and really near.

"Wow."

"Yes, wow!"

Chapter 20

The city lights of Pittsburgh shone in the night sky during the plane's descent as they flew above downtown in a slow loop toward the airport. Cassidy smiled as the plane leaned slightly as it turned and she got an even better view. They'd be landing in about ten minutes so they were quite low.

She had called her father on Thursday and very anxiously asked for an additional loan. Art was quite unhappy when he heard that she was in Chicago and needed two nights in a hotel plus transportation home. Cassidy didn't want to tell him she was moving over the phone. A big announcement like this needed to be done face to face. She promised him that she would explain everything when she got home, and that she'd work out a repayment plan to start quite soon. Art graciously called the front desk of her hotel and extended her stay by two nights, although she did have to change rooms. And then he called his travel agent to book her a flight out of O'Hare. However, he had her fly into Pittsburgh as it was $100 cheaper than Erie's tiny airport. Cassidy tried to point out that it was an hour and a half drive from Meadville, while the Erie Airport was much closer to her apartment, but Art reminded her that would give her time to explain herself in the car. Cassidy couldn't lie, that was more than fair.

After a quick descent and a bit of a bumpy landing, Cassidy found herself walking down the jetway and into the airport terminal. She followed the herd toward the baggage claim. While she had only a carry-on, that was where she had promised to meet her dad. However, when she arrived in the large baggage claim area there was a familiar face waiting for her, but it wasn't her father.

"Alex?" Cassidy asked as she walked towards her eldest brother. Alex was leaning against the coffee kiosk which was currently closed as it was a few minutes after 9PM.

"Oh, hey."

"Hi."

"Did you know you can't smoke in here anymore?"

"I think they have designated smoking areas," Cassidy replied plainly, thoroughly confused as to why this was their opening topic.

"Absolute bullshit."

"It's not that bad. We'll be outside in a minute."

"Don't you have a suitcase?" Alex asked.

"Just a carry-on." Cassidy lifted her small duffle bag.

"Okay," he said, nodding toward the revolving door and walking away. Cassidy stood frozen for a few seconds before running along to follow him outside. The cold air hit her like a brick and she paused a moment to put on the winter coat that she had been carrying.

"Wait, what are you doing here? Dad was going to pick me up."

"Yeah, you're welcome," Alex said sarcastically as he lit the cigarette he had already popped in his mouth.

"Ugh. No. Thank you. I appreciate you coming to get me, I just… I was surprised not to see dad," she explained. Alex took a long drag and exhaled deeply.

"Yeah, dad threw out his back yesterday. He couldn't make the drive. I got nominated because apparently I'm the only one that's awake late."

"Wait, how did dad throw out his back?"

"Um, apparently, he was attempting to chop wood," Alex said. The two shared a look, both trying very hard not to be the first to crack a smile. Cassidy lost.

"Wha -- why was dad chopping wood? He's never done that before in his life," she asked.

"Mom said one of the neighbors was chopping and he wanted to help," Alex shrugged. They both shared a stifled chuckle before they remembered they were mad at each other.

"Come on, it's cold out. Let's get to the car," Alex said, setting off across the crosswalk. Cassidy silently trailed behind as they walked to the parking garage and found his car on the second level. Alex took the final puff of his now stub of a cigarette and flicked it out the window as they rolled out of the garage and he rolled up his window.

"Thank you," Cassidy said, thrilled to not have the March night air circling the car as they went.

"Mmmhmm," he hummed. Cassidy clenched her jaw. This was painful. She refused to ride two hours in annoyed silence.

"Can you talk to me? Please?"

"What?"

"We haven't spoken in weeks. I'm tired of you being pissed at me when you have no right to be," Cassidy huffed.

"No right to be?" he scoffed as he merged onto the northbound lane of the highway.

"That's right!"

"Cassidy… you lied to me for ten years."

"Lied?"

"My sister and my best friend… canoodling behind my back!"

"Ugh! Don't say canoodling. That's gross."

"Well, I call it like I see it."

"But you didn't see it," Cassidy said firmly as she glared at him. "It wasn't a secret relationship. It happened once when you were at work. One time, that's it. We never hung out or talked more than, hey! after that. So stop making up this narrative of an elaborate deceit."

"Oh," Alex mumbled under his breath. If he wasn't driving, Cassidy would have hit him.

"Yeah, oh! You got shitty with me because you misunderstood Laura's drunk ramblings."

"Don't be all high and mighty."

"No, I'm enjoying this. You were a jerk."

"Well, maybe it was a little too easy to believe," Alex grumbled as he changed lanes to pass a semi.

"Why didn't you even try to take my side?"

"Cassidy, your side is still not great."

"Okay, but you made up a whole fake story and got mad about it! That's not fair."

"I guess it was easy to think that way."

"Ugh, you suck," Cassidy groaned.

"I suck, but I'm the one giving you a ride?" Alex challenged.

"I didn't ask you to do that, be mad at dad."

"Jeez! I love you but you are frustrating as hell."

"Well, you won't have to suffer with me much longer."

"What in the world does that mean? Ugh, you're so friggin' dramatic," Alex grumbled.

"It means I'm moving to Chicago!" Cassidy yelled. Alex jolted and hit the breaks. The car swerved and two loud horns blared in anger. "Alex!!" she screamed as he got the car back under control.

"You're what?" he asked in disbelief.

"That's why I was there. I had a job interview, and I got it, and I'm going to move there."

"Why?"

"Why? Because I can't get a job here."

"There are other places!"

"Well, yes, there are."

"Did you and Jake break up and you're fleeing the state?"

"No! Jake will be there, too," Cassidy said.

"You're moving out of state... with your boyfriend?" Alex asked slowly. He was clearly trying to process this surprise information.

"Yeah. And I told Jake I wasn't going to go if I didn't find a job I would love. And I did. The company is great! I'm really excited."

"So, um, what--?"

"So, I got a job, and he got a job, and we found a place to live that's in our budget, and I looked up local organizations and things to do – there's a lot more than I expected," Cassidy rambled. After talking about the public transportation, the restaurants, little beaches on the lake, and the nightlife, she realized Alex was just staring straight out the windshield at the dark road in front of them.

"Care to comment?" she asked.

"I'm just… I can't believe you're leaving." He sounded sad. Cassidy's heart gave a sad thump.

"Yeah," she said in a low voice.

"When?"

"Um, like seven weeks."

"Seven weeks?"

"Yep. My new job gave me time to move – up to eight weeks. But I want to get out there a week early and get a little settled before starting, you know."

"Yeah, makes sense."

"I feel like you want to say something," Cassidy said after a long pause.

"No," Alex replied quietly.

"Alex, a few minutes ago you were ready to throttle me for being a slut."

"Um, no, you were the one ready to do the throttling."

"Fair, but… are you still mad? Are you new mad? Are we good?"

"I'm… We're… I'm going to miss you," he admitted.

"Aw, I'm going to miss you, too. But you have a phone, and I've heard rumors that Illinois also has phones," she teased, desperate to lighten the mood.

"Yeah, I heard that rumor, too," Alex smirked.

"And it's not like I'm not going to still see you," Cassidy said.

"Yeah, but it's different."

"How? I'm--" Cassidy started, but paused mid-sentence. It suddenly hit her. She wasn't going to be at the monthly dinners. She wasn't going to be at all the birthday meals. She would come home for some holidays, but the truth was, she knew she wanted to make her own traditions.

"Cassie?" Alex asked. Cassidy shook her head, not quite sure how long she had zoned out.

"Sorry, I just… I realized."

"Yeah," he nodded, knowing exactly what she meant. Cassidy gulped. As excited as she was for this new adventure, she was sure going to miss the comfortable life she had built at home.

"Ugh, can we turn on some music or you go back to being annoyed with me, or something?"

"I'm not annoyed with you," Alex snapped. They both laughed.

"Who are you going to pick fights with when I'm gone?" Cassidy asked playfully.

"I'm pretty sure I'm the passive one. You, on the other hand…"

"You yelled at me the other week!"

"You yell at everyone every week," Alex countered.

"I'm just passionate! And generally, I'm right."

"Ehhh…"

"You are such a liar," Cassidy sassed. Alex looked over at her and smiled.

"Well, it will be a lot more boring without you," he said sincerely. Cassidy felt the lump rise in her throat once more. She scooted over on the seat to lean her head on his shoulder.

"Thank you for picking me up tonight."

"I'll always pick you up."

"I'm so happy and so sad all at once!" Marissa gushed as she hugged Cassidy tightly.

"I know! Me, too," Cassidy agreed as she hugged her best friend back. Alex had dropped her off from their long journey from the airport about ten minutes ago. Cassidy was happy to be home, but then another wave of sadness hit when she realized it wouldn't be her home much longer. She had called Marissa from the hotel Saturday afternoon after Jake left to drive home and told her the big news.

"We have to do so many things before you go," Marissa began as she pulled back. "We have to go out to a club, we have to get pizza at Ziggy's, we have to go mini golfing at that place off the highway, we have to make tacos and brownies, we have to have a beer at EU with everyone from our floor of the apartment senior year like we did at Halloween. We have to have a night in and rent Jaws! Oh, and--"

"And that all sounds perfect and we have over a month. We can get all of it in, I promise," Cassidy smiled.

"I'll start making calls!"

"It's after 11PM."

"I'll start making a list of people to call tomorrow after work," Marissa said.

"Much better idea."

Cassidy arrived at her parents' house early that Friday. She wanted to talk to her father alone.

"Hi," she called out as she let herself in the front door.

"Cassidy?" Art called from his office off the foyer.

"Yeah," she replied, taking off her coat and hanging it in the

215

front closet and kicking off her boots.

"You're early."

"I know," Cassidy said as she walked into his office. Art was sitting in his wingback chair and reading the newspaper.

"Hey."

"Hey! How's the back?" Cassidy asked, leaning over to give him a hug before taking a seat in the chair next to him.

"Easing up."

"Were you really chopping wood?"

"I was helping Doug Haller down the street."

"Dad, you've never chopped wood in your life!"

"No, but I golf a lot. It's the same thing, a swing is a swing."

"Except the axe is a lot heavier than a club," Cassidy pointed out.

"Oh, you sound like your mother," Art scoffed. Cassidy smiled at him.

"So, dad, I didn't get a chance to talk to you in the car from the airport, but I wanted to tell you: I'll be paying you back."

"I know you will be paying me back," Art said firmly.

"Yes, yes, I know, but I meant soon. I, um… I got a job!" Cassidy grinned. Art beamed proudly.

"You did? Oh, I'm so glad!" he reached over and patted her knee.

"Thanks, dad."

"Tell me all about it! I assume that's why you decided to pull that stunt and go away for a weekend?"

"Well, kind of. See, I got a job as a financial analyst for an engineering firm…"

"Oh wow, great gig. Which company?"

"Franklin Engineering."

"I don't know them."

"Well, that's because they're in Chicago."

"Their headquarters?"

"No, the whole company. I... I got a job in Chicago. I'm going to be moving to Illinois," Cassidy said with a nervous smile.

"You got a job out of state?" Art asked. Cassidy could tell he was trying to figure out how to react.

"I did."

"Well, look at you," Art said with a smile.

"Thanks. I know it's sudden and I know it's crazy, but I think this could be a really good opportunity."

"I'm not going to pretend that I'm thrilled my only daughter is deciding to pick up and leave the state, but I am proud of you for wanting to take a chance."

"It's a big chance," Cassidy said, letting out a deep breath.

"What about Jake?"

"He's going to be there, too."

"Oh, really?"

"Yeah, um... he got a job at Northwestern, and I wasn't sure about what to do, but I ended up getting a job and there's so much to do there, and -- I think it will be a good thing."

"Northwestern, really?" Art asked, looking quite impressed.

"Yeah. Basically teaching and working with the baseball team, like he does at MU, but you know ... more," Cassidy chuckled.

"Well, hot damn."

"Dad," she laughed.

"Do you think he could get me football tickets? I'd love to go to a game."

"Um, I'm not sure, but... probably."

"Who do they all play? I'll need to pick someone good,"

Art said, clearly lost in his football dreams. Cassidy smiled. She would love to have her dad come out for a game. This could be a great tradition for them!

The Banker family was seated around the large dining room table and the serving dishes had finally made full loops around for everyone to fill their plates. Tonight they were enjoying pork barbeque, potato salad, Brussels sprouts, and corn bread. Ellie had joined the monthly dinner, having told Lynne at the wedding that she was really looking forward to it. Cassidy felt a mix of sadness at not getting to watch her full integration into the family chaos, and happiness that she had joined the crew. She was proud to pass the resident girl baton that she had carried for the past twenty-six years over to Ellie. As everyone was digging in, Cassidy decided to take advantage of the momentary silence. She had to pull the trigger.

"I got a job!" Cassidy called out loudly. Everyone looked over at her.

"Took you long enough," Matty smirked.

"Thanks, Mr. Kotter," Cassidy retorted.

"I take that as a compliment," Matty replied.

"You got a job!" Lynne cheered. She stood up, walked around Ben and gave her daughter a kiss on the cheek.

"Thanks, mom," Cassidy said as the rest of the family chorused in cheers of 'Good job!' and 'That's great!'

"Where will you be working?" Ellie asked eagerly. Alex returned to eating.

"I'm going to be a financial analyst at Franklin Engineering."

"That sounds important," Ellie said, looking impressed.

Cassidy took a deep breath to steady herself.

"It's in Chicago."

The only sound was Alex's fork stabbing one of his Brussels sprouts against the plate. It was only a few seconds of silence and everyone staring at her, but Cassidy felt it in her soul.

"Like… Illinois?" Eric asked, his face scrunched as if he were thinking quite hard.

"Yep," Cassidy nodded.

"So, you're moving?" Ellie asked cautiously.

"I am."

"Damn," Matty said, looking surprised.

"When?" Eric asked.

"In May."

"You're missing my graduation?" Ben asked, shooting her a hurt look.

"No, no, I think I'm here for it," Cassidy said, frantically trying to remember if she had budgeted her time correctly.

"May 8th… it's a Sunday," Ben said. Cassidy let out a relieved breath.

"Yep, yep, I'm here. I knew I didn't want to miss it," she told him honestly. She really could never forgive herself if she missed her younger brother's college graduation.

"Who the hell has graduation on a Sunday?" Matty asked loudly before turning to Alex, who had graduated from Mercyhurst seven years prior. "Was yours on a Sunday?"

"Hmmm, I don't think so… I think it was a Tuesday, maybe," Alex said before popping a forkful of potato salad in his mouth.

"Is the motto of the school, we hold graduation on the stupidest day of the week?" Matty quipped. Ellie laughed loudly.

"I think I've seen that engraved somewhere," Eric smirked.

"Shut up," Ben grumbled.

"I'll be there, Ben," Cassidy sat, reaching over and patting his shoulder with her right hand.

"So why are you moving?" Eric asked.

"What about Jake?" Ellie asked.

"Well, he's going, too. He got a job teaching and coaching at Northwestern, and well… it's perfect for him," Cassidy smiled.

"And?" Ellie asked.

"I'm thrilled for him. And I was on the fence about what I was going to do, but I ended up finding a really great job. I like the area, and there's a lot to do. We found a place to live! It just… it's all falling into place," Cassidy shrugged.

"Damn," Matty breathed, looking a mix of surprised and impressed. Cassidy looked over at her mother who was sniffling softly.

"Mom, no, don't cry!"

"No, no, I'm happy, I am, but I'm just realizing this is one of our last dinners," Lynne said, wiping a tear.

"Great job, Cassidy," Matty said sarcastically.

"Mom, guys, I'm not dying! Also, I don't leave for over a month. And after I do, I'll come back and visit, you guys can come and visit me. It will be fun!" Cassidy said.

"I'm sad, but I kind of like that we have an excuse for a road trip," Ellie said with a forced smile. Cassidy smiled at her.

"Are yinz going to be living, like, right downtown? Or don't they have beaches there? Are you living at the beach?" Ben asked.

"Beach?" Art asked, his mouth full of pork.

"Like the ones on Presque Isle," Eric said.

"Oh yeah," Art nodded.

"Well, my office is actually like three blocks from one of the beaches," Cassidy grinned at Ben. "But we found a townhouse in Evanston."

"Where?" Matty asked.

"It's just north of Chicago, top of the city. It's where Northwestern is. So, super close for Jake, he's only like five minutes from campus, tops."

"What about you?" Lynne asked.

"My office is in Chicago, but not far. Jake and I checked the odometer in his truck, it's just over eight miles."

"What's that in city driving time?" Art asked.

"Twenty minutes, but there are buses and trains, too. I'm going to figure it out, guys," Cassidy said.

"Alexander, I can't help but notice you're not super chatty," Matty smirked at Alex.

"I drove her from the airport on Monday. I had two hours in the car to hear all of this."

"And your sister making a life-altering move is boring now?" Lynne asked. Alex sighed.

"No, I'm, it's… good for her."

"Aw," Ellie pouted her bottom lip slightly.

"You're going to miss her," Ben sang.

"Just me?" Alex asked. "Well, that sucks for Cassie."

"We're all going to miss her," Lynne said over the chuckles at Alex's comment.

"There's a spare bedroom in our townhouse -- we can have guests," Cassidy said proudly.

"Alright, tell us about our lodging for when we come," Matty grinned. Cassidy couldn't help but laugh. She talked about their townhouse and the neighborhood they were going to live in, as well as restaurants they had found in the city. As they asked questions and talked and laughed and planned visits, Cassidy felt the weird twisty feeling once again –elated and heartbroken all at once. She had a feeling she would be feeling that a lot in the next couple of months.

Chapter 21

The restaurant was packed and loud, filled with laughter, excited conversation, and the aromas of delicious foods. It was a Sunday evening, the first day in May. The weather finally felt like spring and everyone was out celebrating.

Cassidy sat at a large table with Jake, his mom, Claire, his brother, Will, Marissa, and Brandon. It was Jake's goodbye dinner. He had given his last final exam to his MU students last week, graded them, and finished up his paperwork and notes. He was finished as a professor there. The baseball team had two more games left in the season, but, as they were currently last in the league and Jake had been training his replacement all spring, the clipboard had been passed.

They had spent all day packing up Jake's house. He had rented a U-Haul trailer to hitch to the back of his pickup truck. The house was a flurry of packing. Tape, bubble wrap, wadded up newspapers, and boxes were everywhere. Matty had even stopped over to help for a few hours. However, he had a cookout with his friends already planned that evening and bowed out before they stopped for dinner -- although Cassidy had a strong suspicion that he was simply terrified of Claire and wanted an easy out.

After a full day of boxing and lugging, both the truck bed and the trailer were almost completely full. The only things left in the house were Jake's mattress, which was currently on the living room floor, a table lamp next to the mattress, a few pillows, two sleeping bags, a night's worth of toiletries, and clothes for tomorrow. While the place he had rented during his few years in Erie had never exactly been homey looking, it now looked sad and empty. Cassidy had teared up when they all left for the restaurant.

"This lasagna is delicious," Will remarked as he ate.

"It's so good here, we come all the time," Marissa said as she popped a forkful of ravioli in her mouth.

"Mom's lasagna is better," Jake smirked at his brother. Will rolled his eyes.

"Thank you, Jake," Claire said. "But I know you're just trying to butter me up for once again moving even further away from me."

"Ooof, that had to hurt," Will said.

"It's not like you've stayed close," Jake noted.

"Yeah, but now you're even further," Will sassed.

"You both left. Now shut up," Claire interjected firmly. Cassidy bit her bottom lip in a mix of fear and amusement, while both Marissa and Brandon stifled laughs.

"Will, what are you looking to do now that you graduated?" Cassidy asked, desperate for a subject change. Will had graduated from law school at Dickinson the previous week.

"Oh, that's right, you're a real lawyer now," Marissa said, looking impressed.

"Yeah, I am, sort of," Will chortled. "Um, well I did an internship at a firm in Harrisburg this past year, and they were waiting for my bar exam results. I'm also looking at the Pittsburgh area, as well as around State College."

"When do you get your results?" Brandon asked, taking a sip of his wine.

"Later this summer. It takes like eight weeks to hear back."

"Wow," Cassidy said in deep thought.

"Yeah, so I'm going to take the time and help Jakey move. And then come stay with mom for a bit, and then... well, the test results will tell where I go next," Will shrugged before taking another bite of lasagna.

"How are you holding up, Mrs. Sullivan?" Marissa asked.

"I'm getting by, like usual. It will be strange to have Will back at home for a month or so," Claire replied. She was a stoic woman. Cassidy respected her.

"I can't believe we got everything packed up so quickly," Jake commented.

"You don't have much more than the essentials; that made it easy," Brandon shrugged.

"He is not one for knick-knacks," Will snorted.

"That's good. Cassidy has a lot," Marissa added.

"I don't have that much," Cassidy said.

"Pffftt," Marissa raised her eyebrow. "Cassidy, you have so much stuff. Jake is in for a massive surprise."

"He knows what I have, and it's not going to be as dramatic as you're making it out to be."

"Mmmhmmm. Okay, just wait until you really start packing, then we'll talk," Marissa smirked proudly. Cassidy shook her head. She wasn't leaving for almost two weeks. While she had shuffled a few things in her room, Marissa was

225

right, she hadn't really started packing yet. Once Jake was in their Evanston townhouse, she would have a lot more gusto to pack up and join him.

The six of them spent the rest of the meal talking and joking. Marissa planned everything she wanted to do on her visits, while Brandon argued for the superiority of Indianapolis, but he didn't seem to sway anyone. Will teased that he was going to decorate before Cassidy arrived, and Claire surprised everyone with stories of how messy and terribly decorated her boys' rooms were as children, making everyone laugh. Cassidy relished in every moment of the meal.

Finally, the plates were all empty, and the conversation was starting to lull. They closed out the check and made their way out of the restaurant and into the warm, dark night. There was a small parking lot across the street where they had all parked. This was the moment Cassidy was dreading. Goodbye.

"Oh my gosh, this is it, isn't it?" Marissa asked, pouting her bottom lip.

"Just until you visit," Jake said. Marissa lunged forward and hugged Jake around the middle. Cassidy smiled as he hugged her back. She knew the two of them got along, but hadn't expected them to miss each other with this move. Clearly they would.

Before she could start tearing up, Cassidy turned to Claire.

"It was so nice to see you again. We could not have gotten as much done without you," Cassidy said honestly.

"I do what I can to organize my boys," Claire smirked.

"Clearly, you do amazing work."

"Thanks," Claire nodded awkwardly. Cassidy knew this was a hard moment for her. She glanced over at her friends and saw Brandon gently pulling Marissa off of Jake.

"Come on, he's not dying," Brandon said as he pulled her back and extended a hand to Jake. "It's been fun, man."

"Yeah, great times," Jake grinned as he took Brandon's hand. As they all started talking with Will, Cassidy returned her attention to Claire.

"This is going to be great. Jake really deserves this job, and you know he's going to do so well," Cassidy said honestly.

"Yes, he will… he was always the one I knew would travel the furthest from home."

"Traveling isn't leaving. You'll visit us, right?"

"Will you visit me?" Claire challenged.

"Absolutely!" Cassidy nodded, knowing she was going to need to really juggle the holiday calendar for two Pennsylvania stops on return visits.

"I'll hold you to it."

"I would expect nothing less."

"You watch my boy out there," Claire said. Cassidy gulped, feeling the weight of Claire's request. Though she would never show it, Claire was sad and scared: two emotions she had never expected from this woman.

"He's going to do great. We're going to do great."

"You're fearless, bull headed, and fit for this challenge."

"Thank you?" Cassidy replied slowly, not sure if this was a compliment or not.

"You're welcome," Claire nodded. Apparently, it was meant as high praise. Cassidy tried to feel honored.

"Jake is ready for this, too. He may not be as … bull headed as me, but he put this all together himself. He can be quiet at times, but he's not a scared little boy."

"I appreciate hearing that," Claire smiled. Cassidy returned the gesture. "But I'm counting on you to fight off muggers or murderers or whatever those big cities all have."

"Happy to."

"I knew you would be," Claire said. Cassidy leaned forward and hugged her, despite knowing she was not a hugger. Claire patted her back and stepped away.

"What just happened?" Will asked in a low voice as his mom moved over to talk to Jake. Cassidy grinned at his amused look.

"Your mom and I get each other, that's all." Cassidy shrugged.

"Yeesh," Will sighed, making Cassidy laugh. "What time are you guys leaving tomorrow?"

"Given that we're camping on the living room floor with our mother, I doubt it will be a super fun night. So, I'm guessing we'll be up by six," Will replied with a low chuckle. "Mom's going to want to be on her way back to Johnsonburg the second we're down the street."

"That's fair. At least you guys will be there by early afternoon."

"Yeah. It should be good. I know driving through the city with a trailer will be a bitch, but better than doing it in rush hour."

"The good thing is, it's a straight shot through the city to the north and Evanston is right there."

"Good to know," Will nodded.

"You two won't have too much fun until I get there, right?" Cassidy asked playfully.

"That is yet to be determined. The last time the two of us spent this much time just the two of us was… summer before my junior year -- Jake's senior year in high school. Mom and dad went to Niagara Falls for an early an early anniversary

228

trip," Will hummed, still looking in deep thought. Cassidy laughed.

"Well, the house is still standing, so I'm sure you'll be fine."

"Yeah."

"Have a good trip," Cassidy said, giving him a big hug.

"See you soon," Will hugged her back tightly. They smiled as they pulled back.

"We should go soon, boys," Claire said over everyone talking. Jake walked over to Cassidy and Will took his leave.

"I can't believe it's time," Cassidy said as she wrapped her arms around his shoulders. She could feel Jake snake his arms around her waist to hold her close as they talked.

"Yeah. You're coming out on the thirteenth, right?"

"Of course!" Cassidy assured him, placing a light kiss on his lips.

"I'll call you when I get out there."

"Yes, and give me our new number. Oh my gosh, our new number!" she grinned.

"Yes, our new number."

"And don't kill Will in the car. Or while moving in. He's being very helpful."

"I will not kill my brother in the car. Chicago does have a mob history though," Jake raised an eyebrow playfully.

"You dip, be nice... or I'll send your mom out there," Cassidy whispered.

"Well, shit, you play dirty, Banker."

"If I have to," she smirked.

"I'm going to miss you so much."

"I'm going to miss you, too." Cassidy buried her face in his shoulder for a moment as they hugged tightly.

"I'll see you soon," Jake said, kissing her cheek.

"And call at least twice a week until I get there," Cassidy said, pecking him on the lips.

"Definitely," Jake kissed her again.

"I love you."

"I love you, too," Jake said. They shared a last kiss for a few long seconds before pulling apart.

"Come on, Romeo," Will yelled, was climbing into the passenger's seat of the tan truck.

"Bye," Jake smiled at her before turning to climb into his truck. Marissa lovingly wrapped her arm around Cassidy's shoulder as they watched the Sullivan family drive off. Two weeks, Cassidy reminded herself. In two weeks, she would be with him and they would be starting their new lives.

"Let's go home," Marissa said as the truck turned out of sight at the second light.

"Yeah, let's go." Cassidy smiled at her best friend and they walked to her car with Brandon in tow.

Chapter 22

"Fore!" Ben screamed as the volleyball zoomed diagonally off the heel of his palm, missing Alex's head by an inch.

"This isn't golf," Eric said.

"I thought it just meant watch out," Ben shrugged.

"In golf." Eric shook his head.

"What do you say in volleyball?" Ben asked.

"We say you're an idiot." Alex rolled his eyes as he returned from chasing the ball and tossed it back over the net at his youngest brother.

"Ha-ha-ha. I'm pretty sure this idiot just graduated, with honors, a few hours ago," Ben pointed out before serving the ball once more. This time it flew right to Laura who easily bumped it back. It was Sunday evening and the family was playing volleyball in the Banker's backyard after dinner. The day had been busy and festive after Ben's graduation earlier that afternoon. The whole family, including Cassidy's maternal grandmother and paternal grandparents, sat at the Campus Center to watch Ben and three hundred of his classmates walk across the stage and toss their caps in the air. It was a beautiful, albeit, long day of ceremony that started with Mass, broke for brunch, followed by speeches, and a full commencement program. Lynne burst into tears no less than five times; Ben was the last of her children to graduate. Her youngest baby. She kept reminding everyone that this was the last graduation she would be attending as a mom. While she really hoped to attend future graduations as a grandmother, this was the final time she would be the mother of the graduate. Cassidy honestly felt for her. Five high school graduations and five college graduations. It was the end of an era.

After lots of pictures and hugs, including a few teary goodbye hugs between Cassidy and her grandparents, the eight Bankers, now including Ellie and Laura, departed campus and the city and returned to Meadville. Dinner was a large cookout filled with laughter and arguments. Lynne insisted on cleaning up without help, but Cassidy assumed she just wanted a few moments of peace while they played a spirited game of volleyball in the yard.

"Out!" Art yelled as one of Ellie's returns landed way off to the left. Ellie shrugged, clearly unbothered. While she fit in well with the Bankers, she lacked the competitive spirit and willingness to fight for every point. Granted, that was probably a positive attribute in this environment.

"Alright, my serve," Laura said, twirling the ball in her palms. She served with a thud of her hand and it went right to Matty, who bumped it high. The volley started, one of their longest in the game. Cassidy was just jumping to set the ball over the net when Lynne called out loudly. The ball bounced off her fingertips and smacked Ben in the side of the head.

"Ow!"

"Sorry," Cassidy winced.

"Come on, dessert time!" Lynne yelled. Eric scooped up the ball and they all herded over to the patio where Lynne was setting out trays on the picnic table.

"What's all this?" Ellie asked, looking impressed. Laid out on the table were two cakes and a large plate of about five dozen cookies.

"This is a meaningful night, so we have to have the proper treats."

"Wow, mom," Cassidy smiled as she spotted the cakes. One was decorated with green and white icing and said "Congrats Ben!" with a black graduation cap perched on the C. The other was pink and blue with "To your biggest adventure, Cassidy" written in script. She felt herself tear up slightly.

"Did you make those?" Ellie asked her mother-in-law.

"Yes, I did."

"They look amazing!" Laura said in awe.

"Get a picture, quick! I'm ready to dig in," Art said, a plate already in his hand.

"I know, I know," Lynne said as she picked up the blue, rectangular camera and snapped a picture of the cakes. Then she made Cassidy and Ben stand behind each of theirs and took another snapshot.

Quickly, the cakes were cut, the cookies were loaded onto plates, and everyone took their seats to dig in.

"So, Cass, when are you going to know about football tickets?" Matty asked with a mouthful of cake.

"Honestly, no idea, but I am going to look into it for you."

"Why would we go out to see a Northwestern game? They suck," Ellie scrunched her nose.

"They do, but it would be pretty neat to see a game out

there," Art said, taking a swig of his beer.

"If we want to drive to a game, we go could to Penn State," Ellie grinned.

"Or Pitt," Eric challenged with a smirk.

"Or stay here and watch MU," Laura shrugged, making everyone laugh.

"I think the whole idea is to come visit me and Jake," Cassidy pointed out.

"No, it's definitely the football we're after," Matty quipped. Cassidy rolled her eyes.

"How's Jake doing at the new place?" Lynne asked.

"Good, good. He and Will are there and they haven't killed each other yet, so, that's something," Cassidy chuckled, popping a forkful of cake in her mouth.

"Is he working?" Ellie asked.

"He's shadowing right now. He likes it, but he said he's glad he gets time to shadow before he has to step up as it's a much bigger program."

"When does he officially start?" Alex asked.

"In July for the baseball team and then classes start in mid-August," Cassidy nodded.

"And when do you start?" Art questioned.

"Less than two weeks. I'm leaving early Thursday morning and arrive mid to late afternoon. Then I'll have all weekend to settle in and a few days to really learn my way around a bit. I'm stopping in at the office to turn in my training binders, and I'll start after that!" Cassidy smiled. She felt a mix of excited and overwhelmed. After all this waiting, it was finally happening.

"Wow. And you're not going to be back for a First Friday in… what, like, a year?" Ben commented.

"Yeah, I don't know. I, um, I just need to get through these next couple of weeks first," Cassidy replied.

"We'll see her in less than a year," Lynne said firmly. A chorus of agreement followed. Cassidy appreciated it.

"What about you, Ben? This is your day after all," Laura jumped in, forcefully changing the focus. Ben told everyone about the job he got at a psychiatric facility as an addictions counsellor. Naturally, Matty jumped in with a slew of mad-house jokes that Eric, Alex, and even Laura were quick to build on. Ellie giggled away, especially when Art threw in a joke that absolutely flopped, and Lynne put her head in her hands in embarrassment.

The family talked and laughed well after the sun was down and they were illuminated only by two tiki torches and the dimming patio light that Art had continually forgotten to change the bulb to.

It was after 9PM by the time they were back inside and cleaning up. Other than Cassidy and Ben, everyone else had to work the next day. Once the leftovers had been packed up and distributed, it was time to leave.

Which Cassidy knew was also time for goodbyes. Thankfully she could save three for later. Alex, Eric, and Ben would be helping her make the drive out. Initially it was just going to be Cassidy and Eric; however, after the decision to rent a small U-haul truck for her furniture, it became apparent that none of the family had faith in either of the twins driving a moving truck across town, let alone across multiple states. Frankly, they both found it a little offensive -- even if they were the only two Banker children to have ever had any (thankfully minor) car accidents.

Alex quickly volunteered to help, and Ben, desperate for something to do in his first week post-grad, offered to join on the stipulation that Cassidy bought him a pizza in return. She agreed, though she was a little irritated that no one seemed to have any qualms about Ben driving a truck.

Even with holding off on three of the goodbyes, she still had five painful ones in front of her tonight. Cassidy went to Ellie first.

"Oh, no," Ellie said, pouting her lower lip slightly.

"I know," Cassidy agreed with a sigh.

"I feel like we were just becoming real friends."

"Yeah, the timing kind of sucks." Cassidy gave a half chuckle.

"You're going to tell us all about it and come back and visit, right?"

"Absolutely!" Cassidy assured her. "And you're going to keep me posted on things here and come visit me, right?"

"Absolutely!" Ellie nodded. Cassidy smiled and the two hugged tightly for a long moment.

"Make sure to hold your own at the dinners. You've got to toughen up," Cassidy winked at her as they pulled apart.

"I'll do my best," Ellie grinned. Eric came to stand next to her and nodded at his twin.

"See you bright and early on Thursday?"

"Yes, thank you," Cassidy said.

"Ugh, if it wasn't the last month of school, I'd totally help you," Ellie said.

"It's okay, Matty and Laura are in the same boat. Teachers in the family have to stay until the end of the school year," Cassidy assured her.

"Eric promised to take a few pictures of your new place so I can see it when he gets back."

"Yep, I will," Eric smiled. Cassidy jolted slightly as she felt a heavy arm sling around her shoulder. She was not surprised to see it belonged to Matty.

"Hey, Ellie, what are you going to do while the old man is away?" he asked playfully. Eric rolled his eyes.

"Not too much. I'm having dinner with my friends Friday night and I might go see my parents."

"I get it. That's what you gotta say with him standing right there." Matty dramatically nodded towards Eric. Ellie laughed.

"I'm less concerned with her wanting to throw some random party while I'm gone and more concerned with her going to the animal shelter and adopting some strays," Eric said. Cassidy gasped.

"You're getting a pet?"

"Well, I really want a cat," Ellie admitted.

"Why?" Matty asked, scrunching his nose. He was a dog lover through and through.

"Aw, you should definitely get a kitten. Eric, why won't you let her get a kitty?" Cassidy smacked his shoulder.

"I never said no, we're just getting settled into the new place, still. I'd like to be a bit more organized before bringing in a small animal that we could lose."

"Won't lose a dog!" Matty interjected.

"There are small dogs… some smaller than cats," Cassidy said.

"Yeah, but they're terrible. I mean a real dog," Matty nodded and Cassidy cackled. Eric and Ellie started talking about pet adoption and Cassidy turned her attention to Matty.

"I'm bummed you won't be on the road trip out."

"Yeah… Alex and Eric are going to kill Ben when it's his turn to drive the truck. It'll be funny as hell."

"I can keep Ben in the car with me."

"And ruin everyone's entertainment?" Matty asked in fake surprise.

"I'm more concerned about my worldly possessions strewn across the highway in Indiana."

"Eh, that's fair."

"Please come visit this summer. Jake and I can show you all the cool restaurants we find – you'll love it," Cassidy smiled. She did want Matty to visit, and he was the foodie of the family so would greatly enjoy the huge selection of cuisine in the big city.

"Oh, definitely," Matty grinned. Cassidy turned toward him and gave him a big hug. Their hugs were usually quick or playful -- not that they didn't love each other, but that was just Matty's playful personality. However, this time, he held tight. Cassidy was going to miss him and hated that it would be months until she watched him play another prank. After Matty, Cassidy went down the hall and found Laura. Before she got a word out of her mouth, Laura launched herself forward and hugged her tight.

"Ugh, I'm going to miss you," Laura whispered. There was a catch in her voice that shot right through Cassidy.

"I'm going to miss you, too," Cassidy said as they hugged. There was nothing else she could say. She had known Laura for almost ten years. She had become the sister she'd always wanted.

"You'll call me every week?"

"Definitely," Cassidy assured her. After a long minute, they pulled apart.

"Drive safe, okay?"

"Yeah… make sure Alex gets some sleep before the drive on Thursday."

"I will," Laura smiled.

"Bye," Cassidy said softly before making her way back to where her parents were standing outside of Art's office. She swallowed hard. This was going to be tough.

"Well," Lynne said in a shaky voice as she reached over and brushed a stray strand of hair behind her daughter's ear.

"You guys... um..." Cassidy stuttered slightly.

"We're proud of you," Art said. Cassidy's bottom lip quivered as she looked up at her dad. He looked at her with such pride, yet such sadness. Cassidy could feel that look in her soul. She hugged him tightly.

"Thank you. Thank you so much. For everything," Cassidy cried into his shoulder. He hugged her back. She wanted to say more, but the words didn't come, so she just stayed in his embrace.

Lynne sniffed as she watched them. Cassidy pulled back and looked over at her. She had tears streaming down her face.

"Oh, mom." Cassidy stepped over to hug her. After a long embrace, Lynne pulled back and rested her hands on Cassidy's shoulders and looked her in the eye.

"Cassidy, you be smart out there."

"I will."

"This is such an opportunity and I'm so proud and excited for you, but I'm going to miss you so much," Lynne sniffled.

"I'm going to miss you, too."

"I want you to make a life out there, but I really hope you come home for at least one holiday a year."

"I definitely will. Remember, Jake's family is here, too," Cassidy smiled at her.

"Yes... but don't be running back and forth all the time."

"I won't mom. But I will always come home," Cassidy

assured her.

"Aw," Lynne hummed, reaching up to wipe a tear off of her daughter's cheek with her thumb. Cassidy smiled at the touch.

"You guys are coming to visit at some point?" Cassidy asked, looking tearfully between her parents.

"Absolutely! I want to see you place -- especially after it's decorated," Lynne nodded. Cassidy chuckled slightly.

"Yes, I'm afraid to see what Will and Jake have come up with."

"You'll have time to put your stamp on the place, too," Lynne said.

"We can come out in fall if Jake gets football tickets. Or we can just go in spring – he'll have to get us baseball tickets," Art said. Cassidy resisted an eye roll.

"You can also visit if we don't have a game to go to."

"Well, yeah," Art agreed.

"There are a lot of steak houses out there…"

"Ooo," Art smiled. Cassidy grinned.

"Cassidy, you're blocking us in," Alex said from the front door.

"Coming."

"Well, this is it… you and your brothers drive safe, and call me when you get there," Lynne said.

"Will do. You have the phone number I gave you?" Cassidy asked.

"Yes, it's on the fridge," Lynne smiled.

"Great, alright, bye… Thank you," Cassidy nodded earnestly.

"Goodbye, Cassidy," Art said. Both he and Lynne leaned in and gave her a kiss on each cheek. Cassidy gave a small wave before rushing to collect her purse from the coat tree and departing her childhood home.

She shared a quick goodbye with Alex, she would be seeing him in a few days, and climbed into her Toyota. As Cassidy pulled out of the driveway and headed down the street, she felt tears fall once more. A lifetime of memories was behind her. She wondered when the next time she would get to drive down that street and walk into her parents' house would be. Six months, at the earliest, if they came back for Thanksgiving. It was a weird feeling.

Chapter 23

Cassidy slowly paced around her bedroom at the apartment. It was empty. The carpet showed indents from her bed, dresser, chair, and bookshelf. Her walls were now bare, with a few spots of discoloration from posters that had been tacked up for four years. She crossed her arms over her stomach. The room held so many good memories: lots of laughs, there were many kisses, there were all-night talks on her bed. There was a small black spot on the carpet by the indentation left by her dresser from when she dropped her open tube of mascara when she and Marissa were getting ready to meet a group of friends at a club three years ago. There were memories of music from her boombox playing as she cried after a break up. She could smell the take-out food, the candles, the perfume. This room that had been so filled with life, love, and emotion, was now empty. Cassidy let out a sad sigh as she took one more slow lap around the room. It was time to leave.

She exited her room and made her way down the hall to the kitchen where Marissa was standing at the counter picking at some grapes. She looked stressed.

"So, what are you going to do with my room?" Cassidy asked. She tried to sound casual, though they both felt the heaviness in the air. The guys were all outside getting things organized in the truck. Cassidy had come upstairs for a final look around to make sure nothing was forgotten.

"Dunno. Maybe make it a gym," Marissa shrugged.

"You hate the gym," Cassidy smirked.

"Yeah. Maybe I can do jazzercise or something."

"Please send me a video tape of that," Cassidy snorted.

"Honestly, it'll probably just be my closet," Marissa smiled.

"Excuses for a lot more shopping!"

"I like that."

"So, you're going to be okay here on your own?" Cassidy asked.

"Yeah, yeah. All good… it'll be quiet, though."

"Well, at least Alex won't call in the middle of the night and wake you anymore."

"Not going to lie, that will be nice," Marissa chuckled before a long quiet fell over the two friends.

"So,"

"You'll call me as soon as you get there, right?" Marissa interjected, slowly stepping towards her.

"Yes."

"Like, we don't even have to talk then, but just let me know you're there and then we can talk talk tomorrow."

"I promise, I'll call you as soon as I get in the door," Cassidy smiled. "You have my new number?"

"Yes."

"Will you come out and visit me sometime?"

"Will you come home and visit me sometime?"

"Yes." They nodded in unison, then each let out a small laugh before crashing together is a big hug. They held on to each other tightly. Cassidy took the time to remember the smell of Marissa's apple shampoo and the feel of the old, worn fabric of her favorite T-shirt she wore around the house all the time. "Camp Ramah in the Poconos – Summer 1972."

They were both trying hard not to cry, although tears did slip out. After a long minute or two, they pulled back.

"Don't cry -- you're going to make me feel bad for not being happy for you right now," Marissa sniffled.

"Well, don't you cry either, you'll make me feel bad for leaving," Cassidy retorted with a loud gulp. Suddenly they both let out a sputtering laugh. Cassidy had no idea why, but they went from crying to laughing in seconds.

"Here," Marissa said, walking over to the end table and grabbing a few tissues for them.

"Thanks." Cassidy blew her nose. "You wanna walk down with me?"

"Yeah. I want to see you off. Also, I need to make sure Brandon doesn't jump into that damn truck," Marissa said with an eye roll.

"Oh, before I forget," Cassidy said, reaching into her purse and grabbing her key ring. She fumbled with it a moment before freeing a bronze-colored key with a square head. "Here is the apartment key."

"Hmmm," Marissa hummed as she took the key. "Guess it's really official now."

"Yeah. I can't get back in." Cassidy let out a low breath. Marissa slipped the key into the pocket of her jeans shorts and they departed the apartment together for the final time.

Both the truck and car were fully packed. Both vehicles had their maps in the glove box and the drivers knew where to go. Thankfully, it was pretty much a straight shot. All four Bankers had a bottle of pop and a few car snacks. It was almost 10AM and their goal was to get to Toledo before they stopped for lunch. Knowing the U-Haul was going to need at least one more stop for gas, they still were hoping to pull up to the townhouse in Evanston before 7PM Central time. Cassidy had talked to Jake that morning and he promised to have a feast of take-out options upon arrival. She couldn't wait to see him. Jake assured her that he and Will had not killed each other, and not done any property damage yet. However, one of the dining room chairs apparently took a gnarly tumble and was now down to three legs and half a backrest. Will was determined to repair it, but Jake said it wasn't looking good. The repair project was keeping him occupied, though, so Jake let him continue, with the plan to toss the chair in the dumpster when Will returned home in a few days.

Cassidy hugged Brandon goodbye. She was going to miss seeing him around, but she was glad that Marissa had him to keep her company today. Cassidy and Marissa shared one more big hug. After a final glance around the apartment complex parking lot, she climbed into the driver's seat of her blue Toyota.

Ben was in the passenger's seat, already munching on a bag of BBQ chips. While Ben and Alex were the designated U-haul drivers of the group, they had been squabbling all morning.

Cassidy and Eric decided that, for the safety of all involved and the survival of Cassidy's possessions, they would keep them separated for at least the first leg of the journey. Alex won the coin toss and got to drive the truck first. They would reshuffle drivers after the lunch stop.

Cassidy started up her car, and shifted into drive. Ben popped in her Duran Duran cassette and turned the volume up. Cassidy honestly appreciated the distraction. She led the way for the little Banker convoy as they left Erie and merged onto I-90 West, which was going to be their home for the next seven hours.

About twenty minutes into the drive, Ben had consumed all of his car snacks and was lightly drumming along to the music on his knees.

"Hey, Ohio!" he said. Cassidy looked at the "Welcome to Ohio" sign on the side of the road. She felt her heart thump. She glanced back in the rearview mirror and saw Alex and Eric in the U-haul, and in the far left behind her, she saw the "Welcome to Pennsylvania" sign for passengers travelling the other direction.

"Wow. I really am moving away."

"Well, duh," Ben shook his head before returning to his drumming. Cassidy bit her lip, torn between crying and laughing. Instead, she simply slipped on her sunglasses and smiled.

She'd taken the leap. There was no turning around or looking back. She was ready for her new life, new adventure, and new story to tell!

THE END

Epilogue

Cassidy and Jake

After settling into their townhouse, Cassidy sent her first postcard from the city to her old coworker, Gladys, who had written back immediately. The two remained pen pals for over a decade until Gladys's passing in 2001.

Jake proposed to Cassidy on July 4, 1988 -- their first holiday in their new city. They married on May 19, 1990 back in Erie, surrounded by friends and family.

Cassidy and Jake welcomed son, Dylan Arthur Sullivan, on April 18, 1991 in Chicago.

Jake loved his job with Northwestern -- especially traveling around the country with the baseball team. By the mid-90s he was teaching multiple classes and appointed to the academic board at the university.

Cassidy truly enjoyed her job at Franklin Engineering. She made a large community for herself in Chicago by joining a running club as well as an investment group. True to form, she made friends quickly and happily kept a very full schedule.

Cassidy ran the Chicago marathon in 1993 at age 31. Jake and two-year-old Dylan were happy to watch from the sidelines.

Dylan was a happy and social little boy. He was always involved in T-ball and then baseball from kindergarten through 10th grade. His family from Pennsylvania always attended to at least one of his games each year. He enjoyed the sport, but wasn't quite as in love with it as his parents hoped. He loved building computers and was incredibly intelligent. He got an academic scholarship and attended Penn State – much to

Jake's delight.

Both Jake and Cassidy retired in 2019. With Dylan out of the house, they decide to move back to Pennsylvania to be closer to family. Jake returned as an adjunct professor at Mercyhurst and continues to teach one class a semester. Cassidy is happily retired.

Alex and Laura

Alex and Laura were married on June 10, 1989 in an outdoor ceremony at a park in Erie.

They, reluctantly on Alex's part, moved out their loft soon after the wedding, and bought a house on the edge of the city. Laura was thrilled to have a garden. Alex loved the relaxing front porch, but openly complained about having to shovel so much.

Laura continued to work as an art teacher until retirement 2018.

Alex remained a columnist with the newspaper until he published the first of his five novels in 1995.

They never had children, but love their nieces and nephews dearly.

Matty

Matty continued to work as a high school teacher at Cambridge Springs until retirement.

He had multiple serious relationships over the years, but never married, nor had any interest in marriage.

As always, he continued to enjoy large friend groups and remained very social and active. He enjoyed taking a yearly trip out to Evanston to visit his sister. Cassidy and Jake always took him out to new restaurants and breweries, which he loved.

Eric and Ellie

Two weeks after Eric returned from helping Cassidy move to Illinois, he and Ellie went to the local shelter so Ellie could pick out a kitten: a fluffy black and white cat that she named Doc. Doc was a beloved member of the family for all of his sixteen years. He passed peacefully in 2004.

Eric and Ellie welcomed their first child, a daughter named Rhea Elaine Banker, on May 10, 1992, and two years later, son Cody Aaron Banker on June 29, 1994.

Ellie continued working as a 1st grade teacher until her retirement in 2022, after which she pursued new interest in gardening and baking.

Eric continues his work in HR even today. Ellie jokes that he will never quit and just suddenly die, mid commute, when he's in his 90s.

Rhea has been obsessed with dancing since she was three. She took multiple classes over the years and participated in competitions around the state. In high school she also started to do Pilates and loved it. After graduation she took multiple certification courses and started teaching Pilates, barre, and yoga at a wellness center outside of Erie. She also teaches a jazz class for 10 year olds once a week at her old dance studio.

Cody tried a little bit of everything growing up and enjoyed almost all of it. After high school, he went to the University of Pittsburgh (much to Eric's delight) and got a degree in education. He has a job teaching fifth grade in Butler, PA, a suburb north of Pittsburgh. His college girlfriend got a job in Butler as a physical therapist and they married soon after.

Ben

After graduating from Mercyhurst in 1988, Ben got job at a psychiatric facility in Erie working primarily with addicts.

He worked there for five years before he accepted a job in a small therapy practice in Meadville and worked there until retirement.

Ben reconnected with a former high school classmate, Sherri Nelson, at their five-year high school reunion and they started dating shortly after. Sherri works as an oncology nurse at the local hospital. They married July 19, 1991.

A few years later, they welcomed twin daughters, Shelby Lynne Banker and Abigail Suzanne Banker, born October 1, 1994.

Art and Lynne

Art retired in 1990 from his financial advisor job. Lynne retired in 1992 from her work as a school nurse.

They continue to host family events, including the First Friday dinners, that have gotten significantly more chaotic with grandkids running around. Art and Lynne love spending time with their four local grandchildren, and going to Chicago to see Cassidy, Jake, and Dylan twice a year. Cassidy and her family returned these visits once or twice a year before moving back home permanently in their retirement.

Will Sullivan

After he graduated from Dickinson Law and passed the bar, Will got a job at a law firm in Pittsburgh. Within a year, he started dating Nancy Woods, a woman he kept bumping into at the coffee shop next to his office. Will and Nancy married June 12, 1993 and moved to Cranberry Twp. Will drove down into the city every day for work.

They welcomed their first child, a son named Ross James Sullivan on April 25, 1994, and their second son, Ryan Andrew Sullivan, on August 1, 1997.

Claire Sullivan

Claire remained in Johnsontown all her life. After retirement, she kept busy with a local garden club and a woodworking group.

She enjoys all 3 of her grandsons very much and visits them multiple times a year. However, her favorite is when both of her sons and their families return each summer and there is a week of chaos and fun.

Marissa Solomon

Marissa and Brandon broke up after a disastrous Thanksgiving in 1988.

She quickly packed up and moved to a new apartment in downtown Erie to start over and really focus on her job as an interior designer.

She met Isaac Rosenthal, a bank manager, at a food festival in the spring of 1990. Marissa and Isaac hit it off instantly and started a whirlwind romance. She moved in with Issac that fall, and they quickly married on March 23, 1991. Cassidy happily, though uncomfortably, returned to Erie and stood as her matron of honor, at 8 months pregnant, in a traditional Jewish ceremony. (Calm down -- Jake drove them both ways!)

Marissa and Isaac welcomed three sons:

David Marshall Rosenthal (December 30, 1991), Adam Jonathan Rosenthal (February 28, 1993), and Joshua Samuel Rosenthal (November 1, 1994).

Marissa retired from interior design in early 1994 so she could stay home with her two sons, and then her third. She loved being a stay-at-home mom and felt it was her true calling.

Despite the distance, Marissa and Cassidy remained good

friends over the years. They had a weekly phone call that often lasted hours, and would get their families together at least once a year. Dylan always looked forward to hanging out with David, Adam, and Joshua!

Brandon Calder

After his break-up with Marissa, Brandon quit his job, left Erie, and moved back to Indianapolis with his family to get back on his feet.

He quickly got a new job at an architecture firm in the city.

On a night out, he went home with a woman named Claudia Simmons. She called him weeks later after finding out she was pregnant. Brandon and Claudia never dated, but were able to fairly peacefully co-parent their daughter, Eva Louise Calder, over the years, living less than two miles apart.

Brandon had other relationships, but never married. His focus is always on work and his daughter, whom he loves dearly.

Pete Harris

Cassidy's night club hook up -- remember him? Well, he did finally get to work as a college baseball coach – at Northwestern University. Seriously! Wouldn't that be a fun story to write? Maybe someday. And yes, Cassidy almost passed out when Jake brought her to a team banquet and introduced her to the new head coach.

Pete coached at Northwestern for six years before moving back to his alma mater, Ohio State. He worked there until his retirement and loved every minute of it.

Where are they in 2026?

Cassidy - 64 years old. She has retired from work. Living in Meadville with Jake. Involved in multiple community programs. Very social. Has monthly dinners with Marissa.

Jake - 64 years old. Works as an adjunct professor at Mercyhurst. Living in Meadville with Cassidy. Has converted their shed into a microbrewery.

Dylan - 35 years old. Working in Buffalo, NY as a IT manager.

Alex - After successfully battling lung cancer in 2010, the cancer came back in 2021. He died during surgery in 2023. He was 64.

Laura - 67 years old. She has retired from teaching, but continues working part time at the theater as the art director creating sets. After her husband's passing, Laura created a memorial wall in the hospital garden that she painted with a mural and planted sunflowers all around. She hopes other patients can find peace there. She remains very close with her in laws.

Matty - 67 years old. Matty has retired from teaching. He is active in golfing, fishing, and foodie groups with his large friend group.

Eric - 64 years old. He continues working. Ellie jokes he will never stop. On weekends he will sometimes join his brothers for a round of golf.

Ellie - 64 years old. She has retired from teaching and has gotten into gardening and baking.

Rhea - 34 years old. She works at a Wellness Center as a pilates, yoga, and dance teacher. Her Aunt Cassidy attends her Tuesday morning pilates class every week - a highlight for both of them.

Cody - 32 years old. He works as a 5th grade teacher in Butler, PA. He's married to his college girlfriend. They welcomed their first child in 2024.

Ben - 61 years old. Continues to work as a therapist. Occasionally joins Matty and Eric for a game of golf. Spends most of his free time watching sports.

Sherri - 61 years old. She still works as a nurse, but has started to lessen her hours. Started taking cooking lessons after she and Ben took a trip to Italy a few years back, and loves trying new recipes.

Shelby - 32 years old. She works as an ER nurse at a hospital in Michigan. Shelby is married with two sons.

Abigail - 32 years old. She works as a detective in the Erie police department. Abigail is divorced with one daughter.

Art - Art suffered a severe stroke in 2018. He never recovered and passed two months later. He was 84.

Lynne - 93 years old. Lynne moved into a retirement home in 2022. While she has significantly slowed down and her hearing is poor, she is still sharp and in decent health. She gets visits from her children, grandchildren, and great-grand children multiple times a week, which she cherishes. But she also has friends in the community and plays cards and dominos often.

Final Notes

The monthly First Friday Banker family dinners continued without a hitch over the years. Cassidy made it home for about two a year, but Art, Lynne, and the boys continued them in her absence, though she was missed -- most of the time.

The table got fuller as Rhea, Cody, and twins Abigail and Shelby were born, turning the meals from general squabbles to full-on toddler fueled chaos. Cassidy, Jake, and Dylan's visits only fueled the fire, but watching the five cousins happily play together over the years brought a joy that none of them could deny.

In 2015, Ellie and Eric took over hosting, as it became too much for Lynne. She hated the first few times not hosting, but Lynne came to love "just showing up" quite quickly. Art loved the change instantly.

Now in 2026, the remaining Banker siblings take turns picking up Lynne to come for the monthly meal.

After a couple of decades of First Fridays being full of little kids and chaos, now they are back to just immediate family, minus Art and Alex. Especially after Alex's sudden death, the five Bankers (Lynne, Matty, Cassidy, Eric, and Ben) truly cherish their time together.

However, on the occasional holiday when the entire family is there (which gets harder each year), the chaos brings joy and comfort to everyone around them. Memories of years past.

A firm reminder that it has been a hell of a good life!